ERRATA

Please note the following late changes which were not able to be put into the book prior to publication:

On page x (Table of Contents): The page numbers of the following entries should read as shown:

On page 78 ("All Prophecies Fulfilled"):
The next-to-last sentence should read:

"Two nations had been in Rebecca's womb and the elder would serve the younger."

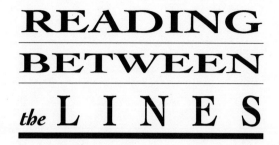

READING
BETWEEN
the LINES

READING
BETWEEN
the L I N E S

NEW STORIES
from the BIBLE

selected and edited by
David A. Katz
and
Peter Lovenheim

JASON ARONSON INC.
Northvale, New Jersey
London

This book was set in 11 pt. Korinna by AeroType, Inc., Amherst, NH.

10 9 8 7 6 5 4 3 2 1

Library of Congress Cataloging-in-Publication Data
    Reading between the lines: new stories from the Bible / David Katz.
Peter Lovenheim.   p.   cm.
    Includes index.
    ISBN 1-56821-604-1 (alk. paper)
    1. American fiction—Jewish authors.   2. Bible. O.T. Pentateuch—
History of Biblical events—Fiction.   3. Fasts and feasts—Judaism—
Fiction.   I. Katz, David. 1953–   . II. Lovenheim, Peter.
    PS647.J4R43   1996
    296.1'9—dc20   96-477
                                                                 CIP

Manufactured in the United States of America. Jason Aronson Inc. offers books and cassettes. For information and catalog write to Jason Aronson Inc., 230 Livingston Street, Northvale, New Jersey 07647.

Contents

JEWISH HOLIDAY STORIES

ROSH HASHANAH

YOM KIPPUR

ACKNOWLEDGEMENTS

We wish to thank the following people for helping us prepare this book: Herb Leviton, for his encouragement; Arthur Kurzweil, for helping stretch our minds far beyond our original idea for this project; Julian Yudelson, for helping us solicit *midrashim* in cyberspace; Joseph Gordon, for computer assistance; Jamie Horowitz, for help in public relations; and Cherie Karo Schwartz, Penina Schram, and Rabbi Norman Cohen for helping us notify potential contributors about the book.

We are especially grateful to our wives, Nancy Katz and Marie Lovenheim, and our children, Emily and Benjamin Katz, and Sarah, Valerie, and Ben Lovenheim, for their support and encouragement.

We also wish to thank Betty Katz, professor of English for over forty years. She gave sage editorial advice. She did not live to see this book in print but we hope she would have been proud.

Introduction

by the Editors

For thousands of years the Bible has fired the literary imaginations of readers from around the world, but the People of the Book have had an especially close relationship to the text. Jews have interpreted, commented upon, argued about each and every word of holy scripture. There has been a love affair with the literature.

For centuries Jews have sought out the meaning of the sacred text by imagining what was happening behind every verse. Stanislavsky called it the *subtext;* Jews have called it *midrash.*

Over fifteen hundred years ago the rabbis began to weave their stories. When the Sun and the Moon were created, the heavenly bodies argued over which would be bigger. When Abraham and Isaac journeyed to Moriah, Satan came to express Abraham's doubts about his mission. When Potiphar's wife tried to seduce Joseph, how did he resist? He quoted her passages from the Bible.

The corpus of texts that came to be known as *midrash* ("seeking out" the meaning) was probably compiled somewhere between the sixth and tenth centuries. In order to interpret and develop Jewish law, the rabbis used stories from human experience to extend the meaning of the text. This literature came to be known as *midrash halacha.* When the rabbis wanted to express a value, make a sermonic point, or teach a lesson of life, they felt free to work and play with the text to make it pour forth its secrets, so that God's revelation would continue even in their time. These stories became known as *midrash aggadah.*

In our time too, Jews have sought out the meaning of God's holy words. What was once a corpus of ancient literature has become a modern literary genre, stories employed by contemporary writers to discover lessons that speak to the present generation. This is a book of modern midrash—an anthology of original works by today's writers and poets.

In this collection, contemporary themes predominate. For example, Jewish feminists have found *midrash* to be the perfect tool to give voice to women in the Bible. Among the many outstanding pieces of this genre included here are those that address violence against women ("The Rape of Dinah," by Barbara Sherrod) women's inheritance rights ("The Daughters of Zelophedad," by Ruth Gilbert), relationships between sisters ("Leah's Eulogy" by Marla Feldman), and a moving tribute to the many named but otherwise unknown women of Genesis ("Genesis *Kaddish*" by Susan Gross).

Men get their chance to contemplate manhood, too. In "Isaac and Ishamel," rabbi and teacher Philip Cohen imagines the estranged half-brothers reconnecting at the funeral of their father, Abraham. In Adam Fisher's thoughtful pair of poems, "Ignored Sons, Favorite Sons," an elderly Isaac wonders if he knowns his own sons any better than his father, Abraham, knew him.

Concern for the natural world is another theme of our writers. In "The First Hamburger," Marc Gellman provides a sizzling answer to the question of why animals stopped talking to people. Peter Lovenheim, in "The Ram at Moriah," suggests the origin of the Bible's many laws against cruelty to animals. How trees protect the environment is explained by teacher Lawrence Kurlandsky in "The First *Kippah,*" found here as a story for Tu Bi-Shevat.

Other contemporary issues addressed include euthanasia ("Why People Took So Long to Die," by Alan Maller), computers and how they affect us ("A New Yorker's Guide to Eden," by storyteller Lisa Lipkin), and strains within a family caused by members becoming more religious, *baalei teshuvah* ("Lech Lecha," by Pamela S. Feldman-Hill).

Whether framed in contemporary terms or not, the essence of *midrash* is to express eternal truths through the writer's personal vision of the biblical text. Our authors deal with timeless and universal themes such as the nature of guilt ("The Shadow," Lucy Schmeidler's insightful story of Cain and Abel), faith ("An Heretical Jonah," by Menorah Lafayette-Lebovics Rotenberg), and the boundaries of human freedom ("Moses and the Fifth Commandment," by David Katz).

When we undertook this collection, we did not know how many writers were producing *midrash* today. Certainly, Dr. Howard Schwartz of Washington University and Rabbi Marc Gellman of

Melville, New York, among others, have made significant contributions in recent years, but how many others were working in this literary form? The response to our solicitation of material was both surprising and gratifying: about one hundred writers submitted nearly three hundred pieces, far surpassing our most optimistic expectations. Most of the authors were not rabbis or religious scholars; they were professional fiction writers, poets, storytellers, teachers, and students. All of which leads us to conclude that *midrash* may be enjoying a renaissance.

What inspires someone to write a *midrash?* Those best able to answer are the writers themselves. We asked all contributors to prepare short pieces to explain what led them to write their *midrashim*. These statements appear at the end of their stories and are often compelling.

The pieces assembled for this book take many creative forms. In addition to short stories and poems, our writers present a letter ("Letter from Isaac," by Linda Steigman) a lullaby ("Jochebed, Mother of Moses," by Barbara Holender), a lawyer's oral argument ("Moses and the Ten Contractual Provisions," by attorney Alan Posner), a treatment for a screenplay ("Cain and Canine," by Joel Grishaver), and a modern-day "rap" ("Aaron's Rap," by Diane Demeter: "Aaron here, Aaron, Yo!/You know the big brother of the main man Mo!")

Our contributors write from some unusual points of view, including that of a dove ("The Dove's Tale," by storyteller Rafe Martin), an idol ("The Material Calf," by Diane Demeter), and the Torah itself ("The Dreams of the Torah," by Rosie Rosenzweig).

The rabbis of ancient days were comfortable with anachronisms (*ein mukdam v'ein m'uchar,* "there is no early, and there is no late"). Likewise, our writers' inventiveness produces some startling anachronisms. These include Adam and Eve crunching numbers at a computer ("A New Yorker's Guide to Eden," by Lisa Lipkin), Noah deconstructing a chair to its electrons ("A Dove's Tale" by Rafe Martin), Lot's wife running from Sodom as she tries to remember if she unplugged the iron ("Lot's Wife," by poet Margaret Kaufman), and a group of Israelites chanting knock-offs of 1960s protest songs ("Sing a Lively Song" by Peter Lovenheim).

The book is organized according to the key verse taken from the five books of Moses. A group of stories at the end is arranged according to the Jewish holiday cycle.

Rabbi Eugene J. Lipman, of blessed memory, who was a friend and mentor to both of this book's editors, once explained that *midrash* "results from the zeal of Jewish scholars to squeeze out of Torah all truth." Would the Torah not rejoice that so many people today are rediscovering through *midrash* a personal relationship with the text? Through *midrash,* every Jew is given poetic license; every Jew has the freedom granted by tradition to be inventive, to play with holy words.

A New Yorker's Guide to Eden

by Lisa Lipkin

And the Lord God commanded the man, saying, 'Of every tree of the garden you are free to eat; but as for the tree of knowledge of good and bad, you must not eat of it; for as soon as you eat of it, you shall die.

—Gen. 2: 16-17

And God, being a hopeless romantic, knew life wouldn't be any fun without a moon. So God made a moon, and it glowed in the sky. But it needed something to howl at it, so God made a coyote. God tried a variation on that animal and came up with a dog. But the dog needed something to chase, so God made a cat. It was naughty and whimsical and delightful so God made a larger one— a tiger. And larger still, a lofty lion! . . . then an elephant!! . . . and a dinosaur!!!!! And, when done with the large animals, God made the small ones: ants, grasshoppers, bees, mosquitoes. And because God knew that one day there would be a place called New York City—cockroaches.

But the moon looked lonely in the sky, so God created stars to keep it company. And they twinkled and glistened next to the moon. They were so enchanting God wanted to create something that was special and could understand and appreciate their beauty. That's when God invented Man. A handsome fellow named Adam, whose big eyes took in every drop of life.

But quite honestly, how long could Adam swing from the trees, or feed the monkeys, or walk the dogs? He was getting bored. And he was lonely. So one night, when the sky sang with moonlight and laughed with starlight, Adam made a wish upon those stars. He said, "I wish for a human companion, someone with whom I can share this beautiful place, someone who'll tan with me on the beach." That's when Eve popped into the picture. She was lovely and the two belonged to each other and Adam wasn't lonely anymore. They would run through the high, sensuous grasses, dance among hot-pink roses and speckled pansies, dig their toes into moist patches of emerald dew. They would play games like Hide and Go Seek, Leap Frog, and Scrabble. And they would revel in this glorious paradise called Eden. Until, one day, trouble came.

Adam was off gathering food for dinner. Eve was sitting on the edge of a rock, humming, when she was abruptly interrupted by the sensuous *ssssss* of a seductive silver snake.

"Ssssay there Eve, what are you doing?"
She was taken off guard. *"Well, uh, I was practicing my middle C in the forest."* The snake slithered up and addressed her with the finesse of Mae West.

"Sssssssay there Eve . . . why don't you follow me inssssstead?"
Like the Pied Piper, whose music lured unsuspecting lads to war, so Eve felt herself seduced by the snake's serpentine sounds. She followed the snake behind a long skinny tree. Although the tree was only an inch in width, as soon as they moved behind it both the snake and Eve disappeared from view. Like a safari leader, the snake whisked aside wild branches with its tail as it led Eve deeper and deeper through paradise. They finally came to an area where the foliage thinned. The snake slithered up ahead and wrapped itself around a large object nestled in a group of redwoods. As Eve approached, the snake offered her its coveted object. It was an alluring, shiny, brand new Apple computer.

"Say there Eve . . . why don't you try this Apple?" He pulled up a stump and motioned for her to sit. The keypad seemed overwhelming at first; she didn't know what to do. She cautiously pressed one key, then another, then another. It was music to her. She found herself pressing and pressing away like a composer creating a symphony, like a chef inventing a perfect meal. Faster and faster she rode the keys like a sailor on the high seas. Within the hour she had learned how to type a résumé. She had mastered Word Perfect 6.0. She'd faxed. In short, Eve was obsessed.

Meanwhile, poor Adam didn't know Eve had gone and was very worried. He found himself asking animals if they had seen her. All but the aardvark were helpful. But it was to no avail. By dusk, he was frantic. He started to make a small fire in their usual spot when suddenly, he too was lured by the strangest sound. *"Sssssssssss sssssssssssssssssss"*

He rode its resonance to Eve, who was busy typing.

"Why Eve, it's Adam, your man! He was noticeably ticked off. *"I've been worried about you!!!!"* But Eve was not in the mood for him, not at that moment. She was deep into new programming. *"Oh be quiet Adam, please! I'm trying to figure out the maximum number of animals we can catch within the smallest given radius."* And she kept typing away. Adam didn't know what to do. But the snake did. *"Sssssay there Adam. Why don't you try this Macin-tosh?!"* And it, too, was enticing, like a ripe piece of fruit. And Adam too, became obsessed.

From that time on, all Adam and Eve wanted to do was work on their computers. In the morning they would throw on their three-piece fig leaves and run to their cubicles in the woods . . . the woods in which they no longer took joy. The savory scent of pine needles would surround them. But they didn't take time to smell them. The balmy air would caress their skin, the sun would embrace them with golden light. But they were too busy to indulge. And at night, when the stars twinkled in the sky and the moon covered them in moonglow, they were too tired to notice. And in this way, they could never again return to the Garden into which they were born.

AUTHOR'S NOTE

I finally bit the bullet a few years ago and bought my first computer. It was a magic box that cast its spell on me. I became more and more ensnared by its seemingly infinite possibilities and spent hours in front of my personal tree of knowledge. But there was a price to pay—a price, I'm convinced, we will all pay as technology usurps our time and interpersonal connections. "A New Yorker's Guide to Eden" is one of the original stories I perform on stage in a show called Who Towed Noah's Ark? . . . my own interpretation of Bible stories told through the voice of a modern city girl. Creating *midrash* in this way has been enormously helpful to me, not just as an artist, but as a Jew, living in a crazy city, trying to figure out how I can maintain my Jewish identity here or anywhere in the Diaspora.

Forbidden Fruit

by Marla J. Feldman

And the Lord God commanded the man saying, "Of every tree of the garden you are free to eat; but as for the tree of knowledge of good and bad, you must not eat of it; for as soon as you eat of it, you shall die." The Lord God said, "It is not good for man to be alone; I will make a fitting helper for him." . . . The two of them were naked, the man and his wife, yet they felt no shame.

—Gen. 2: 15-18, 25

The Garden was lush and green, filled with the voices of nature, unafraid. I lay down in the tall grass and closed my eyes, lulled by hypnotic chants . . . crickets singing . . . elephants bathing . . . antelope racing . . . chimps playing . . . my stomach growling. I opened my eyes and looked up. There, dangling above my head, was perfection. Ripe. Red. Beckoning. Ready to explode off the vine. I reached up lazily, half asleep, my mind foggy from the Day, yet vaguely unsettled. . . . I plucked it. (Or did I catch it as it fell?) I took a bite. Joy! As its juice dripped from my cheeks, its coolness coated my throat, filled my belly, sated me. What pleasure!

Suddenly my eyes shot open. A spark. An awareness. This was the forbidden fruit! I bolted up. I understood, felt, knew . . . We no longer belonged in our ignorant bliss.

Adam approached, smiling, lustful, admiring my naked body in the sunlight. As he drew closer his expression changed. A frown of concern. Fear. I smiled to reassure him. I took his hand. I placed my fruit in his palm and curled his fingers around it. He looked at me. He looked at the fruit, dripping with blood-red juice. Like a child, his eyes begged a question, pleaded with me to explain. I urged his hand to his mouth. He shared the fruit of knowledge.

5

Once again he gazed into my eyes. With tears he surveyed the Garden of his childhood. He said good-bye to the friends of his youth. I took his hand and led him home.

ADDITIONAL REFERENCE

When the woman saw that the tree was good for eating and a delight to the eyes, and that the tree was desirable as a source of wisdom, she took of its fruit and ate. She also gave some to her husband, and he ate. Then the eyes of both of them were opened . . . —Gen. 3:6-7

AUTHOR'S NOTE

"Forbidden Fruit" resulted from a "guided meditation" with a *havurah.* Reflecting on the weekly Torah portion, we closed our eyes and imagined ourselves in the Garden of Eden. Why did I eat the fruit? How did I feel? What was I thinking? These are the questions I tried to answer in my *midrash.*

Through *midrash,* we discover new meanings in our ancient scriptures and find ourselves in the text. In creating *midrash,* I endeavor to engage our ancestors in dialogue, searching for their unspoken words. I write *midrash* to understand better my heritage, my God and myself.

The Parable of the Serpent

Anonymous

Now the serpent was more subtle than any beast of the field which the Lord God had made.

—Gen. 3: 1

In the beginning, God didn't make just one or two people. God made a bunch of us. Because God wanted us to have a lot of fun, God said, "You can't really have fun unless there is a whole gang of you." So God put us in this playground place called Eden and told us to "enjoy."

At first, we had fun just as God expected. We played all the time. We rolled down the hills and waded in the streams. We climbed in the trees and swung in the vines and ran in the meadows. We frolicked in the woods. We hid in the forest and just plain acted silly. We laughed a lot.

Then one day this serpent told us that we weren't really having fun because we weren't keeping score. We didn't even know what "score" was. When he explained it, we still didn't see the point. But he said he would give an apple to the one who was best at play. And we'd just never know who was the best if we didn't keep score. Well, we could all see the point of that. Each of us was sure of being the best at play.

Things were different from then on. We yelled a lot. We didn't laugh so much. We had to make up new scoring rules for the games we played, and games like frolicking we stopped playing all together. It was just too hard to keep score.

By the time God found out about our fun, we were spending forty-five minutes a day in actual playing and the rest of our time working out the score. God was very upset about that and said we couldn't use the garden anymore if we didn't stop keeping score. God shouldn't have gotten upset just because it wasn't the kind of fun God had in mind. But God just wouldn't listen and kicked us out and said we couldn't come back until we stopped keeping score.

To rub it in, or get our attention, God told us we were all going to die anyway, and our score wouldn't mean anything. But God was wrong. My cumulative all-game score is 16,548-½. That means a lot to me. If I can raise my score to 120,000 before I die, I'll know I've accomplished something in my life. And even if I can't, my life has a lot of meaning now because I've taught my children to score high. And perhaps they will be able to reach 200,000, or even 300,000.

Really, it was life in Eden that didn't mean anything. Fun's great in its place, but without scoring there is no reason for it. God has a very superficial view of life, and I'm sure glad my children are out being reared away from God's influence. We were lucky to get out. We're all very grateful for what the serpent taught us.

AUTHOR'S NOTE

"The Parable of the Serpent" appeared anonymously in *The World of the High Holidays, vol 1,* edited by Rabbi Jack Riemer (Miami: Bernie Books).

Paradise Lost—
For Better or Worse?

by Marlena Thompson

So the Lord God banished him from the Garden of Eden to till the soil from which he was taken.

—Gen. 3:23

Adam was bent low, harvesting the corn that he had planted in the spring. He wiped the sweat off his face as he pulled up the last ear and placed it in the large basket Eve had woven for just that purpose. He gazed at the impressive pile of corn with more than a little pride. He had worried so about this crop! He was afraid that it would wilt in the summer heat. But he had watered it well. And he had harvested the corn before it had become overripe, even if it meant spending the last few weeks in the field, just to make sure.

"Well," he said aloud with no small sense of self-satisfaction. "Not bad for a man who didn't know corn from cabbage just a few short years ago!"

"True, not corn from cabbage . . . nor an apple from opportunity either!" said Eve as she approached Adam, balancing a water jug on her head with one hand and holding her toddler's small hand in the other. She gave Adam the jug, urging him to drink. She sat down upon a large stone and lifted her baby onto her lap.

Adam drank deeply. When he was through, he tossed the jug aside and stared at his wife, saying,

"Eve! How can you make light about eating that apple? How can you call it 'an opportunity'?" He looked nervously over his shoulder. "Do you want something else that's terrible to befall us?"

"And just what terrible thing has befallen us, Adam?" Eve spoke gently for she was feeding the baby, whose name was Cain, and didn't want to disturb the feeling of calm within her during these moments. "How can you ask, 'What terrible things'? Why, look at my face!"

"I am. You look quite handsome with a suntan. Field work suits you, my husband." Eve looked at Adam with affection, clearly enjoying her own playfulness.

"Be serious, Eve. My face is wet from perspiration from the hours of work I've put in. It's just as God told me. I remember the words exactly: 'By the sweat of your brow will you eat bread.' Adam's voice softened as he watched the sweet scene before him, that of his wife, lovingly feeding his first born. "And though it's true, Evie, that you do make the best corn bread this side of Paradise, I've got to work pretty darn hard to get that bread—planting, tending, harvesting."

"Oh, is that all," murmured Eve. Having fed the baby, she was well pleased to hear him release a resounding burp.

"No, that is *not* all," sputtered Adam as he tended to do when Eve did not seem to get his point. It was evident that she was not seeing it now. "As a matter of fact, I can name another 'terrible thing' that involves *you.*"

Eve's look of surprise told Adam he needed to explain.

"Why, it was less than a year ago when you screamed blue murder, saying things I'd rather not repeat—the day this little devil was born!" Adam tousled the few hairs on his son's head.

Eve rocked her son to sleep with a lullaby that one of the sweet singing birds had taught her back in the days of Eden. As she rocked her child, she said to her husband in a clear, strong voice:

"Adam, look at that basket filled with beautiful yellow corn. I saw how proud you were when you pulled that last ear from the ground. And well you should be. God created corn, to be sure, but it was *you* Adam, who brought it forth from the earth, sweat of your brow and all! True, back in the days of Eden, all you needed to do was pluck a fruit off a tree, but that was a child's game! Don't you think you'd have grown just a tiny bit bored with the same kind of life after a century or two?"

"Well, what about you?" asked Adam. "Don't tell me that you enjoyed giving birth to that little one. I was there, remember. I heard your screams. I recalled what God said to you: "In pain you will bring forth children." Is not pain a terrible thing? Can you still call eating that apple 'an opportunity'?"

"Yes, and yes, my dearest husband. Yes, pain is a terrible thing. But, perhaps I cherish this little one all the more because I suffered so to give him life. For just as you need to sweat and groan to bring forth fruit from the earth—work that you value—admit it, I shall need to feel pain to feel the greatest pleasure of all: to give life. Pain might be a curse, but motherhood is a blessing!"

Adam frowned just a bit and said, "Well, to hear you speak, one would say that our expulsion from the Garden of Eden was no great loss."

"Not so. It was a tremendous loss. A loss of innocence. But, come close, Adam. Look at this child. He is yet innocent and unknowing, just as we were in the Garden. When he is hungry, he does not worry. All his needs are satisfied, just as ours were in the Garden. But this child will grow. He will grow and he will *choose.* And he will have to live with the consequences of his choices. Our legacy to him, Adam, is opportunity, don't you understand? The opportunity to choose his own path in life. Would you wish this child to remain as he is now, all his life, without understanding, without knowledge, without reason?"

Hoisting the basket of corn onto his shoulder, Adam smiled and said, "Evie, I can almost taste that wonderful corn bread of yours. Speaking for myself, man was not meant to live on fruit alone, don't you agree?"

ADDITIONAL REFERENCES

Unto the woman He said: "I will greatly multiply thy pain and thy travail; in pain thou shalt bring forth children . . . —Gen. 3:16

And unto Adam He said: " . . . In the sweat of thy face shalt thou eat bread . . . "—Gen. 3: 17, 19

AUTHOR'S NOTE

As the Judaic Program Coordinator of a small Jewish day school, I provide the teachers and parents with a study sheet for each Torah portion. I write original *midrashim* in order to clarify various points under discussion. I wrote this particular one to counter the common conception that Eve was responsible for introducing pain and drudgery into the world, much as Pandora was responsible for unleashing a multitude of woes into the world. By focusing upon a different perspective, I hope to have introduced a different perception of both Eve and the loss of innocence.

Eve

by Barbara D. Holender

. . . when they were in the field, Cain set upon his brother Abel and killed him.

—Gen. 4:8

One son lies on the ground
not moving
the other stands apart
with dirty hands.
Neither one speaks.

I see them every time I close my eyes.

Look at your hands!
Say something.

> *I don't know . . .*
> *I didn't mean it.*
> *Abel, get up.*

> *Mother?*

Mother, what, Mother?
Make it unhappen?

What are mothers for?

AUTHOR'S NOTE

The story of Cain and Abel is a stark tragedy that opens wide areas to interpretation. The first death was a fratricide—in the text, a matter between Cain and God. Abel is merely the victim, never clearly presented. And where were the parents? Only afterward, we learn that they made another child to "replace" Abel. (Gen 4:25)

The tale begs for some human emotion. What must Eve have felt, coming upon the scene? How could Cain understand what he had done? What does death mean? And why can't mother make everything right? In these questions, I found my *midrash.*

The Shadow

by Lucy Cohen Schmeidler

*Hevel was a keeper of sheep, but Kayin was a tiller of the
ground. In the process of time it came to pass that Kayin
brought of the fruit of the ground an offering unto the Lord.
And Hevel, he also brought of the firstlings of his flock and of
the fat thereof. And the Lord had respect unto Hevel and to
his offering; but to Kayin and his offering He had not respect.
And Kayin was very wroth and his countenance fell. And the
Lord said to Kayin, "Why are you wroth? and why is your
countenance fallen? If you do well, shall it not be lifted up?
and if you do not do well, sin lies at the door; and its desire is
for you, but you may rule over it." And Kayin spoke to Hevel
his brother. And it happened when they were in the field that
Kayin rose up against Hevel his brother and killed him.*

—Gen. 4:2–8

He was always there, my brother, like a shadow. "Kayin, my little
man," Mother would say, hugging me, and Hevel would be standing there, watching, saying nothing. What did we need him for?

When I farmed the land as Father taught, Hevel would watch,
copying everything I did, until I yelled at him to go away. Then I
would be free of him for half a day.

At those times, he took to wandering in the hills with the sheep
and goats, and came back smelling like them, too. He learned to
take milk from the goats, shooting it in a stream into his mouth.

He appeared one day looking strangely pleased with himself,
dressed in a garment he had made from twisted bits of sheep's
hair. He claimed it was better than the skin of a dead animal,
lighter and more comfortable, and even offered to make similar
clothes for the rest of us. Mother and Father were speechless, but I
took him aside and explained, very patiently, the wrongness of

15

changing what our Creator had given us, until Hevel finally stopped smiling and went off again.

About that time, I got the idea of showing my thanks to our Creator by setting aside some of my crops as a gift. And if Hevel took note, I thought, so much the better. Let him see who was the man between us and who the shadow. For it was I who did real work, raising food for us to eat, with some to spare.

I cleared away the weeds and soil from a large flat rock and spread on it some grain and vegetables, a token only, for I knew the Creator doesn't need food as we do. Then I spoke over it a few words of thanksgiving, and left it.

By and by, Hevel came home. He was very much interested in what I had done and asked a lot of questions, ending with whether I thought our Creator would be pleased by a present from his flocks.

"How are they yours?" I asked, astounded. "Did you plant and water them?"

"I find water for them," he answered seriously, "and pasturage, and I chase the wolves away."

"Well then," I said, humoring him, "perhaps the Creator would like a present."

Hevel's face lit up. "I must give God the best. Young Curly, I think, who is developing such a fine coat, and Black Face, whom I had planned to start milking . . ." He went on like that, talking about the various sheep and goats, while I controlled myself and waited. Finally, when he went out, I decided to follow.

It was a longer walk than I had expected, and Hevel chattered all the way. When we reached the flocks, he walked right in among them, pausing now and then to look one over, or to shake his head and go on. At last, when he had selected several animals, he began to lead them away from the main herd, while they stupidly tried to run back and others tried to join them.

When he had managed to separate his chosen animals from the others, he led them a long way by paths only he seemed to see, until we stood at the top of a narrow path leading steeply down to a valley. I wondered, if he led the animals down there, how he would ever manage to get them back up. Here Hevel stopped and stood talking a long time to our Creator, giving thanks for the use he had been permitted to make of the goats and sheep, as well as for everything else he seemed able to remember.

I didn't quite see what he did next, but suddenly one and then all of the animals were leaping down the path into the valley. The sun must have come out from behind a cloud just then, because I remember closing my eyes from the light, and when I looked again, the path and the valley were empty.

I don't remember returning home. I had a dream that night in which the Creator chided me for being angry, and warned me against sin.

Well, I was angry. I had never blamed Hevel for being born second or not being much of a farmer, but for him to act as if he were the important one was more than I could take. I tried to speak to him, but what could I say?

The next day I went to my fields as usual. My offering still lay as I had left it, only looking somewhat wilted. I worked as hard as I could, trying to force everything else from my mind, but nothing went right, and I found myself pulling up vegetables as often as weeds.

And then Hevel came along, as happy as I'd ever seen him. "How's it going?" he asked.

"I'll show you," I said, pointing behind him, "look over there."

And then I picked up a digging stone and hit him as hard as I could on the back of his head. And kept hitting him, after he fell, until my arm was too tired to continue.

He was perfectly still. He had never cried out, and now, when I knelt to look at him, he lay as one asleep, but with no sign of breathing. I shook him gently and called his name, but he showed no more life than the carcass of an animal.

I realized with horror what I had done. And yet, almost at the same time, I had a feeling of freedom. For he would never again follow me around; I would never again have to look at him or hear his voice.

But I have no freedom. Over and over in my sleep, I go through it again, only in my dream I am the one killed, without time to cry out. And while I'm sure the killer isn't Hevel, I never see his face.

But that's not the worst of it. A dozen times a day I half hear footsteps behind me, or half glimpse someone over my shoulder, and I turn to see no one. For we were brothers; from the day of his birth I was never alone, and the memory refuses to die. And now it is this absence, this void, that shadows me wherever I go.

AUTHOR'S NOTE

I write *midrash* for two reasons: as a way of reaching a better understanding of the Bible; and as a writing exercise. Because the basic plot is provided by the biblical text, the challenge is to provide full characterization and motivation. This particular *midrash* was written for the New York Midrash Writing Workshop (previously of The American Jewish Congress's Martin Steinberg Center for Jewish Artists, now unaffiliated).

I wrote "The Shadow" because I was intrigued by the fact that the only witness and survivor of the killing of Hevel was Kayin. So, if there was any lesson to be learned, it was Kayin's lesson, and therefore his was the best perspective from which to view the incident. I always like to look at familiar stories from the viewpoint of someone who is integral to the event but dismissed as "too insignificant," "too evil," and so on, to pay attention to.

Cain and Canine

by Joel Lurie Grishaver

And the Lord said unto Him: "Therefore whosoever slayeth Cain, vengeance shall be taken on him sevenfold." And the Lord set a sign for Cain, lest any finding him should smite him.

And Cain went out from the presence of the Lord, and dwelt in the land of Nod, on the east of Eden. And Cain knew his wife; and she conceived, and bore Enoch; and he builded a city, and called the name of the city after the name of his son Enoch.

—Gen. 4:15–17

When you try to sell a story to Hollywood, you always have to pitch it in just a couple of sentences.

Here is my pitch: Jack London writes a *midrash* on Cain; it is sort of "White Fang Meets the Fugitive." After the murder, Cain asks God for a sign to protect him from being lynched. Being ironic, God assigns Abel's guard wolf to protect Cain, even though the wolf wants to kill him, too. It is the perfect buddy picture.

It is late at night. I am working past the "I must go to bed" point—getting ready for another "Dawn of the Dead"—when it happened. Tomorrow, or is it this morning, I have to give a lecture on how the *yetzer ha-rah* can be *tov me'od*. The Bible is running through my Moviola in a blur. I am carefully reviewing the footage, getting ready to write my lesson. I am running the text back and forth, high speed and slow motion, when all of a sudden one of the splices breaks. I hadn't been expecting splices.

But there I was with a broken piece of film. In one hand I was holding this piece of text:

Adonai put a sign on Cain—so whoever met him would know not to kill him. Cain left God's presence. He came to camp in the land of Nod [homelessness], East of Eden.

That should have been the end of it. Cain had blown it. God had done the vengence thing, and the scene should have faded to black. That's what it always did when they told it in Hebrew school. Cain becomes a fugitive, wanders the earth like Dr. Richard Kimble, working as a bartender one week, as an elementary-school janitor the next. He gets to do a good deed or two. Then, his identity is discovered and he has to run. Despite the good deeds, no one is seriously going to believe that he saw a one-armed man fleeing from the scene of the crime. The story was not supposed to have a happy ending. But then, I looked in my other hand and saw the continuation.

And Cain knew his wife. She got pregnant and gave birth to Hanokh. He [Cain] became a city-builder, and he named the city after his son. Hanokh fathered Irad. Irad fathered Mehu-ya-el. Mehu-ya-el fathered Metusael, and Metusael fathered Lamekh. Lamekh took two wives: one was named Adah and the other was named Tzilah. Adah gave birth to Yaval. Yaval was the father of all who live in tents and herd cattle. His brother's name was Yuval. He was the father of all who play the harp and the flute. Tzilah became the mother of Tuval-Cain, the one who forged all tools of copper and Iron. Tuval-Cain's sister was Na-amah.

I took out a loop, examined the break in the film, saw the glue and suddenly discovered that these two pieces of Genesis had once been spliced together. And by deductive reasoning—the Sherlock Holmes thing—it became clear that part of the text was missing. A piece was clearly missing. Someone had removed it. In one of my hands, cursed Cain was supposed to wander the earth alone—always fearful of losing his life. In my other hand was a story, new to me, but there in the Torah for all to find, of Cain becoming the father of a big clan, surrounded by a loving family, with clever children who designed the first Metropolis. If it wasn't for Cain, there would be no major league teams, no NFL, no major Museums, no Symphonies, no Tower Records, and probably no Jazz, nothing more than Delta Blues, and definitely no Rock 'n Roll. It was new to me, thinking of Cain as the progenitor of Metallica. What else do you get when one man fathers both the first metalsmith and the first musician. Suddenly, Led Zeppelin was biblical.

Humming "Stairway to Heaven," I contemplated the missing sequence. I opened a few books, found one *midrash* that listed seven different possibilities about what "The Mark of Cain" could have been. The last one I remember was that "The Mark of Cain" was Abel's sheepdog. Then I must have fallen asleep. As I dreamed, the Moviola in my mind screened this *midrash*.

Long shot: From a crane, looking down, we follow a pool of blood through the trampled wheat. It leads to Abel's head. He is dead. We continue a few inches along the ground, see the bloody rock. The wheat is deep yellow. The blood red stands out. Suddenly, we hear barking. The camera pulls back, and we see a dog standing guard over the body. We see Cain in a crouch, facing the dog. His hands are up to protect his face.

Cut to a medium shot of the Dog: We see the teeth. The saliva is dripping. The bark is deafening. The dog is just days past being a wolf. The dog is just a few hours tame.

Cut to XCU of Cain: We see his face through his protective hands. There is blood on those hands. There is blood splattered on his face. He has been crying. We see terror, too.

Cut back to the Dog: His legs flex. He is ready to leap.

Cut to overhead shot: Cain falls back. Then God's voice calls out. It has no physical reality. Cain answers, trying to sound calm, but he keeps on looking at his dead brother and at the dog.

Cut to the helicopter shot: Cain and the wolf head off together. They start walking away. The man walks, the wolf circles, sometimes ahead, sometimes behind, always annoying.

Dissolve into night scene: The wolf sits in the dark. By him is a big fat rabbit he has brought down. He is chewing and snarling. Behind him, in the dark, we see a campfire burst into flames. Cain is standing over it, blowing and then fanning it. He has a small, scrawny rabbit, which he roasts.

Cut to the Wolf: He tears a bite out of his fat rabbit and growls at the man. You can hear him say, "Mine's bigger!" You can hear him say, "Stay on your side or I'll tear you limb from limb."

Change depth of field: We blur past the wolf to focus in on Cain. He smiles at the roasted meat. He rips off one leg, tastes it, and says "good." He breaks the rabbit in half, and tosses half of it to the wolf.

Change depth of field: We focus back in on the wolf. He noses the meat, tries to ignore it, then sneaks a bit. He sits back down on his hinds. He thinks for a minute, then takes his rabbit over to the man. The man cooks it; the wolf looks on carefully. When it's done, Cain carefully puts it back on the ground and steps away.

Zoom In on the Wolf: He moves slowly towards the meat, then eyes Cain. Moving almost faster than the eye can see, the wolf lunges at the meat, snaps the fat rabbit in half with one bite, then raises his head and howls. He is silhoutted by the full moon. Then, he takes half of the meat and retreats to his place. The man grabs the other half of the rabbit and moves to the other end of the fire.

This is where the montage begins. Bryan Adams begins to sing new lyrics to the song he recorded for both *Robin Hood* and *The Three Musketeers;* it should work for this film, too.

Morning. Wolf and Cain both head into the river. Each makes a big deal out of splashing into the water, proving that he can take cold.

The wolf catches a fish. Real suave. Cain tries it and falls on his ass. The wolf puts his fish on the rock, moves next to the man and catches another. The man gets it, and uses the stand-still-then-drop-like-lightning-from-above technique. He holds up his fish, and says, "This time, mine is bigger."

Man and wolf cross the mountain. The wolf outscurries the man, stopping to wait for him at each crag. The man, meanwhile, gives him a needed push to get him over a jump that is too high for him.

Man and wolf do a tug of war with a fish, both wind up falling into the water.

Man lights fire. Wolf brings two rabbits.

Snow falls, Cain and the wolf sit under a crag. Cain tries to light a fire. The wood is too wet, the wind too strong. The wolf wimpers. Cain opens up his arms. The wolf growls. Cain says, "I don't like this either." The wolf crawls towards him. Cain opens his coat, and he and the wolf huddle for warmth, back to back. The wolf growls. You know he is saying, "Stay on your side." Cain says, "And watch what you are dreaming about, too!" Dawn finds then sleeping arm in paw.

We then see a couple of guys in the editing room. One of them says, "I get it, Cain and the wolf tamed each other."

The big confrontation: Cain goes to the well to draw water for the two of them. Five guys surround him. They start to beat on him. The wolf jumps in. They fight, then run. They limp out of town together. The wolf is badly hurt. Night falls, Cain sneaks into town to get the water the wolf needs.

The love scene: The wolf sits in the dust. A woman comes out for a night walk under the stars. She is singing. The wolf joins in. She finds and pets him. Cain comes back. The wolf softly bites the woman's hand and places it into Cain's.

Cross-dissolve: Cain and the woman are still holding hands. Twenty years have past. They are now in a city. Their grandson *Tuval Cain,* unveils his new metal sculpture of the wolf. Bryan Adams starts to sing that same song again, and the credits start to roll. The best boy is *Metusael.*

The phone rings. I'm late for a meeting. Again, I've fallen asleep at my computer keyboard. I fall into the shower and try to figure out whatever happened to the missing part of the Cain story.

Why did someone censor it? Then I smile, thinking of the kid who tore out this page of the story, like we tear pages out of a phone book—not to censor it, but because he felt that he needed it. I wonder: How many good myths did the Xerox machine save for posterity?

On the TV, which ran all night, Timmy and Lassie are busy getting the kitten out of the tree.

In class today, I'm supposed to explain how the *yetzer ha-rah* can be *tov Me'od . . .*

AUTHOR'S NOTE

Cain and Canine happened almost the way the *midrash* suggests. Writing a book on gender and Jewish spirituality called *The Bonding of Isaac,* I was working on the Jewish application of Robert Bly's notion that a "marking" is a necessary ritual in male initiation. Then I read an article by Rabbi Brad Artson on *kashrut* and vegetarianism in which he glossed the *midrash* that a dog was one of the "marks of Cain." At that point, I hit my head and this story emerged full-bown.

Why People Took So Long to Die

by Allen S. Maller

All the days that Adam lived came to 930 years; then he died.

—Gen. 5:5

Why did people live so long in those early generations? Or, to put it more exactly, why did people take so long to die in those early generations?

At first, the Angel of Death was a doctor. Even though people suffered greatly from illness and infirmities the Angel of Death refused to end their lives. He believed that life was sacred and that people had no right to end it even for themselves. Thus, Adam lived for several centuries in a convalescent hospital. His son, Seth, was in a coma for over four centuries, and his son Enoch was senile the last six centuries of his life. Although people pleaded with the Angel of Death to take them sooner, he delayed their deaths for centuries with the most advanced technology then available.

Enoch was 243 years when Adam died. Enoch was a righteous man who walked with God. He had been praying for Adam to die for more than a century. Each time he returned from visiting Adam in the convalescent hospital, Enoch begged God to order the Angel of Death to do his duty. When Adam finally died Enoch thanked God and composed a special prayer: The *kaddish*. Although the *kaddish* is a mourner's prayer, this is why it does not mention death at all.

Enoch was worried that, like everyone else, he would live too long and end up without dignity and, God forbid, in pain and agony. He wanted to spare his children and grandchildren the agony which the generations that had preceded him had faced.

Enoch protested to God continually. After Enoch walked with God for 300 years, God took him. Since the Angel of Death didn't take him the Torah does not say "he died" but "he was no more." The Angel of Death did not learn from this that more years are not better years and indeed the Angel of Death dragged out the death of Enoch's son so he suffered more than any other man. For Methuselah lived 969 years until he died.

It was the women who finally merited the first victory over decrepitude. The sons of God (holy men or angels) saw how good and humane women were and how they cared for their parents during their parents' centuries of decline. Even in those days, daughters usually honored and supported their parents more than sons did. Men took women for granted until they found themselves competing for wives with the angels. Because women would find it much easier growing old with (and taking care of) angels rather than old men, God said, "My spirit shall not abide in man forever, because he is flesh, and his days shall be 120 years." Yet although God had declared a maximum lifespan the Angel of Death refused to act accordingly. So kindhearted and liberal was he that he found all kinds of ways to avoid killing people.

Noah, who lived during this generation, also was a righteous man. He was so pained by the long-term suffering of his decrepit ancestors that he refused to have children. This spared them the anguish of watching him decay into a shadow of himself. Noah was almost three times as old as his father, Lamech, when Noah first became a father. Although for generations people had been praying for death to come sooner, the Angel of Death had resisted. He feared that he might act too soon and be blamed by others later.

However, when the flood occurred, the Angel of Death saw how peacefully and happily all the people over 400 years old greeted death. Thus, in the generation of Noah's grandchildren and for the next two generations the Angel of Death cut the life-span maximum in half and people were spared the last four to five centuries of decay. People were so overjoyed at this that the Angel of Death cut the life span maximum by another 50 percent for the next three generations.

People were still happy at this, but some began to worry. True, 239 years (as Peleg lived) was still too long. But two more 50 percent reductions would leave only about 60 years maximum. And that seemed too short. If a man exercised regularly, observed the dietary rules, studied Torah, and always listened to his wife, he could be vital, and live for 70 years. With good luck perhaps a decade or two more.

When Nahor died at 148, his grandson began a protest. However, the Angel of Death, having started down the slippery slope of judging life by its quality, would not be deterred. Indeed, he became so aggressive that for the first time people were cut off prematurely—even children before their parents, as it says of Abraham's brother, "Haran died in the lifetime of his father Terah."

Now the Angel of Death struck sooner and sooner. Abraham's great grandson, Joseph, died at the age of 110. Even more frightening, the Angel of Death began to teach people to sacrifice their babies in a fire to Moloch. And even though God made an example of Abraham's test and told him "Do not raise your hand against the child, or do anything to him," human sacrifice became widespread.

So, God had to intervene. When Israel received the Torah at Sinai, it contained the commandment not to follow the other nations' "abhorrent act that the Lord detests of sacrificing sons and daughters in fire to their Gods." Because the first Angel of Death had become so extreme, he had to be destroyed and replaced with a new one. The second Angel of Death took the life of Moses at the age of 120, "while his eyes were still undimmed and his vigor unabated."

Since the death of Moses the maximum life span has stopped decreasing. The second Angel of Death ended people's lives when they were in severe pain or decline, reasonably and mercifully, taking the middle path between life at any cost and death for any reason.

ADDITIONAL REFERENCES

And all the days of Enoch were three hundred sixty and five years. And Enoch walked with God, and he was not; for God took him.—Gen. 5:24

And all the days of Methuselah were nine hundred sixty and nine years; and he died.—Gen. 5:27

And it came to pass, when men began to multiply on the face of the earth, and daughters were born unto them, that the sons of God saw the daughters of men that they were fair; and they took them wives, whomsoever they chose.—Gen. 6:1–2

And the Lord said: 'My spirit shall not abide in man forever, for that he also is flesh; therefore shall his days be a hundred and twenty years.—Gen. 6:3

And Peleg lived thirty years, and begot Reu. And Peleg lived after he begot Reu two hundred and nine years . . . —Gen. 11:18–19

And Nahor lived nine and twenty years, and begot Terah. And Nahor lived after he begot Terah a hundred and nineteen years . . . —Gen. 11:24–25

And Haran died in the presence of his father Terah . . . —Gen. 11:28

So Joseph died, being a hundred and ten years old.—Gen. 50:26

When the Lord thy God shall cut off the nations from before three, whither thou goest in to dispossess them . . . be not ensnared to follow them . . . for even their sons and their daughters do they burn in the fire to their gods.—Deut. 12:29–31

And Moses was a hundred and twenty years old when he died; his eye was not dim, nor his natural force abated.— Deut. 34:7

AUTHOR'S NOTE

I enjoy studying the *midrashim* of our sages because it is fascinating to see the creative ways in which they make the wisdom of the past relevant to issues of the present. I write *midrashim* to make my contribution for future generations.

In our generation, the extremist spirit of the first Angel of Death has reappeared. Some people are suffering prolonged deaths, being artifically fed and treated when there is no reasonable hope of returning to health, and other people are sacrificing lives through abortions because they don't want a boy or a girl baby. I wrote this *midrash* because understanding the Angel of Mercy's middle path between ''life at any cost and death for any reason'' will be increasingly important for those who face the difficult decision of when actively to end a life.

The Flood: A Dove's Tale

by Rafe Martin

And it came to pass at the end of forty days, that Noah opened the window of the ark which he had made. And he sent forth a raven, and it went to and fro, until the waters were dried up off the earth. And he sent forth a dove from him, to see if the waters were abated from off the face of the ground . . . And the dove came in to him at eventide; and lo in her mouth an olive-leaf freshly plucked . . .
—Gen. 8:6–8;11

Memo from Noah:

The impassioned and cryptic piece of writing below was found by me when I was cleaning up the ark some weeks after we had come to rest on Mt. Ararat. I have to confess how much it surprised even me. I had thought that the raven had failed and the dove alone succeeded. Such, I now see, are the erring ways of humankind! I now believe that the raven was the truly profound one. So deep a creature was he that, when he saw the branch, he saw only Divinity itself. His darkness was truly bright! The dove's wisdom was the wisdom of the everyday world. In that realm, we can simply pull up a chair, sit down on it, and eat a meal or talk to a friend, whatever we like. It is the comfort found in the appearances of things. But when raven is shown a chair before he sits, he begins meditating on the nature of the person who made it. In an instant he knows whether the maker was left or right handed and discerns his or her innermost thoughts. Next he enters into a meditation on the flow of the wood's grain and discovers in its patterns many secrets of the created universe. Going deeper yet he arrives at the realm in which that solid-seeming, physical chair, which stands serenely in our world, is itself a vast, universe of whirling electrons, positrons, tachyons, atoms. Going further still, he attains the sphere in which the chair remains immoveably rooted in the Original Divine and Unnameable Emptiness. So profound is the raven that he would, in this way, moving from rung to rung, in the end be completely immersed in Awe of the present moment of Creation itself. The Divine waters lap around him. What chair, then, would he need?

In each of us there is a raven of unlimited profundity and a dove of delight in surfaces. Both are necessary for a whole and mature life. And why, you might ask, is this? Because in God's wisdom it was meant to be so.

The Flood: A Dove's Tale

Finally things became so bad, people were so lost in the minutiae of things—all respect for the sacred Ground, the Source of life forgotten—that God broke the seals and loosed the heavenly waters. Then Divinity poured down, flooded the earth, the low places, high places, people and all creatures. All were buried beneath the waters of the Godhead. Nothing, not a single separate *thing* was visible. Except the ship and, in it, the last and first man, Noah, his family, the generating animals, and, in them, the seeds of all differing potential.

The waters shimmered in Glory, all separations swallowed up Eternally. Was there Time? What was Time? Forty days and nights are Forever.

Then Noah brought up out from the bowels of the ark a dark, glistening raven. Great raven stretched his wings and with power-ful beats set forth croaking over the splendid deep, a lone speck dwindling, dwindling and gone. Depth responds to depth and, when raven returned, eyes blazing, he had found Nothing. Not a thing. How could he? To the deep there is only *depth*, only the great flood of Divinity—and that is all. Then Noah sent me. I had not raven's depth. Fragile and pale as the light playing on the surfaces of things, I launched myself out over that shimmering plain, flat, featureless as glass. Over the great calm expanse, I flew—and flew. Clouds were mirrored on the divine waters below.

And I saw my own breast and wings reflected, hovering, in those lambent waters.

I flew to the end of the world, to the end of all things, where all things begin. And there at the tip of a tiny peak found—difference!—found branching, new life! The world of time and change had re-entered Eternity! This, the gift of my shallowness. Ah, such indescribable joy in a gnarled branch, a green leaf, a black fruit. How it glistened, sparkling with a fervor to *be*. To be what? And what was it? I had no name for it and so flew back, back over the tedium of Glory, hallelujah, to the ship, the peak, the man. Who fed me, stroked me, let me rest. Named it *Olive*, "peace." The waters of divinity receded around us. We had found the ordinary again. Selah.

And so the life we know once more began.

AUTHOR'S NOTE

These days, we readily confuse literal historicity with truth. We have forgotten the meanings of stories and think they need to have simply occurred to be "real." When our narratives become so literalized, we begin to think we must defend details in our stories against those found in the stories of others. This fundamentalism, a loss of imagination, causes untold suffering. *Midrash* is a wonderful vehicle for reopening the doors of possibility. Creating a *midrash* for the story of the Flood allowed me to explore spiritual dimensions potential to the tale. The raven and the dove each offers us a unique perspective on our own lives. And as for the Flood itself, perhaps it was not simply a downpouring of literal water. In commenting on, recreating, and personalizing a story through *midrash,* one can examine all possibilities.

The First Hamburger

by Marc Gellman

And God blessed Noah and his sons, and said to them, "Be fertile and increase, and fill the earth. The fear and the dread of you shall be upon all the beasts of the earth and upon all the birds of the sky—everything with which the earth is astir—and upon all the fish of the sea; they are given into your hand. Every creature that lives shall be yours to eat; as with the green grasses, I give you all these.

—Gen. 9:1–3

Once, animals talked just like people. Once, every living creature ate only grass and nuts and a few berries when it could find them. No living thing ever thought about killing another living thing to eat it, until the day Noah wanted a hamburger.

One night Noah dreamed of a hamburger. When he woke up, he wanted one real badly. But Noah wasn't exactly sure how to get a hamburger, so he asked his friend the cow: "I dreamed about a hamburger last night. Do you know where I can get one?"

The cow gave Noah a puzzled look and asked, "What's a hamburger?"

"I don't know exactly," Noah replied. "All I know is that in my dream the hamburger was something delicious—between two buns with lettuce, onions, pickles and some special sauce."

"Have some more grass and forget about it," said the cow.

Noah asked the snake, who was the smartest of all the animals, "What's a hamburger and how can I get one?"

The snake whispered in Noah's ear, "To get one you have to make one."

"I don't know how to make one." Noah sputtered.

The snake laughed, pointed at the cow who was peacefully munching some grass, and said to Noah, "To make a hamburger, you have to kill that cow, chop up her meat, and fry it in a pan—or flame broil it!"

Noah's mouth opened wide, "But . . . but . . . the cow is my friend! She is a living thing just like me! I can't kill her, chop up her meat and fry it in a pan! And what is flame broiling anyway?"

By now the snake was rolling around on the ground laughing, "Kid, if you want a hamburger, that's what you gotta do."

Well . . . Noah really wanted a hamburger and so that's what he really did! The first hamburger tasted delicious. But when Noah came again to the fields everything was different. When he walked towards the birds, they flew away. When Noah went over to say hello to the cows and the sheep and the buffalo, they ran away from him. Even the fish swam away when they heard Noah coming.

Noah could not understand what had happened to his friends the animals, and he could not find one single animal who would explain it to him. In fact, since the day when Noah ate the first hamburger, no animal has ever talked to a person. They are still too angry.

AUTHOR'S NOTE

In the biblical text, we can observe that, from Adam to Noah, people are not allowed by God to eat meat, and that when it is allowed, it is clearly a concession by God to the carnivorous appetites of human beings, not a moral virtue. The first chief rabbi of Israel, Rav Kook, drew from this the lesson that vegetarianism was by far the preferable diet for a pious Jew.

The Sign: a Midrash of the Rainbow

by Cherie Karo Schwartz

I have set My bow in the cloud, and it shall be for a token of a covenant between Me and the Earth.

—*Gen. 9:13*

Noah and his family stepped out from the ark into the first sunshine they had seen in forty days and stood upon land. When they saw the clean new Earth, Noah and his family wept for joy. God wept with them. The sky wept a sun shower of tears as God spoke to Noah and his family, saying:

"I am *your* God who brought you forth into this new land. Look around you and see the cleansed Earth. Listen and hear the sounds of animals and the wind moving through the trees. The world is once again new. I know the world cannot always be this way; it does not seem to be human nature to always be good. But you and the generations to come after you can try."

Noah was willing to do whatever God asked of him.

God continued, "I will make a covenant with you, the first of the world's new people. I will give you a sign that I am with you, one that will remind you that the world was created in peace and then re-created in peace, to remain so for all time.

"The sign will be a bow that fills the heavens, an arc of light. But this will be a new light, one that shines through the waters of a flood or a rain or tears. This light will show all the colors of beauty that can fill your lives as you live in peace."

Then God bent toward the Earth with a mighty hand and an outstretched arm and made an arc across the sky. And just where the hand of God had been, there was a sheltering band of every color spread out across the clear blue sky.

First red, for the blood that gives people life.
Then orange, for the flames of warmth that brings com-
fort, and for the fire of the soul.
Yellow, for the sun which helps all things grow, in the full
light of day.
Green, for grass and trees, and the plants' new life.
Blue, for the sky and the sea, connecting heaven and
earth.
Indigo, for the dawn and the dusk, at the beginning of the
day and of the night.
And violet, for the deep night, when the world rests and
renews itself.

Noah and his family gazed at the beautiful arc of light, watching the rainbow flow from one end to the other. They saw it touching near and far, bridging sky and ground.

And then Japheth, Noah's youngest son, asked his father, "We came full circle in our journey on the ark, from dry land to water and once again to dry land. Why doesn't the rainbow come full circle?"

Noah puzzled over his son's question. He looked up to study the arc of colors in the sky. Then he answered:

"Perhaps the rainbow is a sign. Not all things are yet full circles. God has begun the work by making the arc in the heavens. Making the arc come full circle here on Earth will be our work."

And so it remains.

ADDITIONAL REFERENCES

But Noah found grace in the eyes of the Lord.—Gen. 6:8
Noah was in his generations a man righteous and whole-hearted; Noah walked with God.—Gen. 6:9
Thus did Noah; according to all that God commanded him, so did he.—Gen. 6:22

AUTHOR'S NOTE

Midrash is an opening. Sometimes while studying text, a turn of phrase will hold me transfixed, open to ever-widening circles of interpretation. This is the moment of the *midrash:* reconnecting with the deep well-spring of our ancient stories; re-creating the *ruach* (spirit). So it was for this *midrash,* "The Sign." A teacher-friend asked me to evolve a new approach to the Noah story. I read the text with new eyes. First, there was the vision of the brilliant-colored rainbow. Then there appeared two seminal questions. Beyond the science, why these colors? And what message awaits us? So, the story continues.

Lech Lecha

by Pamela S. Feldman-Hill

Get thee out of thy country, and from thy kindred, and from thy father's house, unto the land that I will show thee. And I will make of thee a great nation, and I will bless thee, and make thy name great; and be thou a blessing . . .
—Gen. 12:1–3

"Get thee out of thy country, and from thy kindred, and from thy father's house . . ." Who is this god that calls to you, Abram? Who is this god who would tear you from your home, from your family? From me? Have I not been a good mother to you, my beloved Abram? Like this god of yours, have I not also admonished you to move forward by yourself, and for your own sake? I am proud of your inner faith and conviction; I have fostered this in you, but, oh! how these lessons return to haunt me now!

This god promises to make you a great nation, and to bless you. Have I not also blessed you every night since you were a child, rocking you in my arms, sharing with you the stories, the language, the blessings of my people? You are *my* blessing, my son; is this not enough? Must you also be a blessing to this mysterious god?

As you go forth into this strange land, as you are challenged by this new and fearsome path, I am left here alone and trapped in the land of our ancestors with emotions that well up inside of me. My tears overflow with the melodies of your childhood, the memories of your youth, the mention of your name.

I watch you leave to build the life that you claim will be my heritage, with visions of a world I cannot comprehend. I do not understand why you bear an obligation to this new god, or why this obsession must lead you to where you will be a stranger in a land that is not yours. I share the pain that your decisions bring, and your struggles tear through my soul. I fear for you. Is building your home in this new and untamed land truly your destiny, or are you merely being obstinate?

Even as a child you pushed against me to take your first steps, unsteady but determined, and I knew that too soon I would watch your path turn away from me, your back growing smaller into a night illumined by countless stars.

In pain I will watch your struggles and with wisdom I will let you go. But fear not, my beloved son Abram, for as you will always be my blessing, so will the love of your mother always be your shield.

"And Abram went forth as the Lord had commanded him . . ."
Genesis 12:4

ADDITIONAL REFERENCES

And He said unto Abram, "Know of a surety that thy seed shall be a stranger in a land that is not theirs, and shall serve them . . ."—Gen. 15:13

And He brought him forth abroad, and said, "Look now toward heaven, and count the stars, if thou be able to count them," and He said unto him, "So shall thy seed be."—Gen. 15:5

The word of the Lord came unto Abram in a vision, saying: "Fear not, Abram, I am thy shield, thy reward shall be exceeding great."—Gen. 15:1

AUTHOR'S NOTE

As a Jewish artist, my work has become an arena to explore biblical characters and stories as archetypes for contemporary behaviors. This has led me to the study of ancient *midrash* and to the development of my own "visual *midrash*" through my paintings.

"*Lech Lecha*" was written as a corresponding text to a painting inspired by a friend's *aliyah* to Israel. As I observed the pain and pride of her family and friends, struggling to understand and respect her religious choices, I was inspired to reflect upon Abraham's mother and her thoughts as she watched her son depart.

Hagar Talks Back

by Barbara D. Holender

*Sarai, Abram's wife, had borne him no children . . . So
Sarai . . . took her maid, Hagar the Egyptian . . . and gave
her to her husband Abram as concubine . . . and when she
saw that she had conceived, her mistress was lowered in
her esteem.*

—Gen. 16:1-4

Did you really expect me
to be your surrogate?
You act like you own me—
show me the contract that says
'To be redeemed on presentation of bearer
one manchild for Sarah and Abraham
with love from Hagar.'

Ishmael is mine;
I bore him fair and square.
No use to call me uppity maid,
it was your idea. But let me tell you, lady,
that was no business deal, the way your husband
fondled me and stroked my thighs.
He never once called me by your name.

        (Oh that was good; try it again;
        don't lose your nerve.)

Did you really expect . . .

AUTHOR'S NOTE

In reading with my Bible study group (a *minyan* of women), I was struck by how little had been said about some very interesting, independent-minded women. These women became my friends —I felt that I knew them. *Midrash*, especially in monologue, gave them a chance to speak for themselves. Hagar, whose barren mistress Sarah was "lowered in her eyes," would surely have had the words to talk back, even if in no position to do so. But what a temptation! I saw Hagar as the first surrogate mother, in a dilemma only too recognizable today.

Lot's Wife Encased In Salt

by Robert B. Barr

*As the sun rose upon the earth and Lot entered Zoar, the Lord
rained upon Sodom and Gomorrah sulfurous fire from the
Lord out of heaven. He annihilated those cities and the entire
Plain, and all the inhabitants of the cities and the vegetation
of the ground. Lot's wife looked back, and she thereupon
turned into a pillar of salt.*

—Gen. 19:23-26

In his haste for safety, Lot did not realize what had happened. He
thought perhaps his wife was simply lagging behind once again
and had not heard his questions. So Lot called louder: "How are
you doing? Are you holding up? Can you keep on going?" But
again his questions were met with silence. Concerned now that his
wife was not answering, Lot realized he needed to turn back to
look for her, but he feared what might befall him if his eyes were to
look towards the horizon.

Carefully, Lot turned his body around keeping his eyes cast
to the ground. He only allowed his eyes to survey the ground,
conscious that one skyward glance would be his last. As he looked
about, all he saw was ground made smooth by the constant blowing of the wind and a lone salt formation that rose oddly from
the earth. Again and again he looked. Each time, the results
were the same: his wife had disappeared and only a salt pillar
broke the desolation.

Slowly, Lot began to realize what had occurred. His wife had
looked back. Cautiously, Lot walked to the pillar of salt. He looked
closely and saw his wife encased within it. From her appearance it
looked as if her punishment had come swiftly. His wife looked
caught in flight, now frozen for all time.

Carefully, Lot studied the woman whom he had loved in life and now loved in death. Though they had been warned, Lot could not believe that for a simple glance back, his wife would had been taken from him. He was angry that such a minor infraction would warrant such a harsh and drastic punishment. Though he cursed this injustice, he knew that there was no turning back the clock. Once his wife had been taken by death she would never return.

Her skin looked translucent as the sun sank slowly behind her. Lot's once-vibrant and energetic partner was now silent and still. Though they had known difficult times and their voices had been raised more than once in anger with one another, a bond of love had been woven between them. They had shared much: the joys and frustrations that life offered, the intimacy of loving partners, the challenge of being parents. Their lives had been enriched by companionship. And though his wife now stood next to him, Lot knew he was now alone.

Lot wondered what his life would be like now that the woman he loved would no longer be there to calm his fears or hold him when he was afraid. Her judgment, upon which he often relied, would no longer be forthcoming. That special warmth they shared would no longer exist. Lot knew that with his wife's death, a portion of himself had died as well.

It was unfair that the one who helped complete his life had been taken from him without just cause and now he was alone. Lot was not sure he could forge the future without her; he was not certain he even wanted to. Sorrow gripped his heart. Grief wrapped his soul. The pain he felt was beyond any he had known before.

He remained next to the pillar for some time. He stroked it and touched it, as if to reconnect himself to his wife trapped inside. He pondered his future. He knew that all he needed to do was lift his eyes to the horizon and the pain he now felt would be eased forever. His grief would cease, his sorrow would end, and he would stand once more with his wife.

To look back or to rise, moving forward into the future, was now the challenge that Lot faced. He was not sure what was more difficult. With a heaviness in his soul, Lot realized that a future still lay before him, that he should not turn back.

He looked upon his wife for a final time as he prepared to continue his journey. A tear fell upon his cheek and perched upon his lip. Lot tasted, and it was salt.

AUTHOR'S NOTE

The death of a loved one is surely one of the most difficult challenges we face in life. At that moment, we struggle to understand even as we gird ourselves to continue living. Writing "Lot's Wife Encased in Salt" allowed me to explore, within the context of this biblical story, one person's thoughts and feelings as he looked upon his wife for the last time. We, like Lot, carry within us the memories of those who have touched our lives even as we face the future and journey forward.

Lot's Wife

by Margaret Kaufman
(After Akhmatova)

But his wife looked back from behind him, and she became a pillar of salt.

—Gen.19: 26

They had no time—the just man
hurried across the bridge,
followed God's magistrate
along the black ridge.

His grieving wife lagged behind
as if she had no will,
arms heavy with useless things,
heart heavier still.

She couldn't recall if she'd shut the door,
turned off the iron; worse guilt,
she'd left behind the baby pictures,
her mother's ring, her wedding quilt.

One arm raised as if to gather
her whole life in that embrace,
tears blurring the view,
without much thought she turned her face,
became what she had shed. Who grieves
for this nameless woman, Lot's reflective wife?
I grieve.
I know holding on can cost a life.

AUTHOR'S NOTE

Midrash, as a form, is connected to Torah. But poets and writers often draw upon texts from literary traditions and use them, as students of Torah use midrash, to consider life and loss, what it means to exist in community or in isolation from it. Russian poet Anna Akhmatova drew upon Lot's wife because it spoke to her. Although effectively silenced by the Soviet government for forty years, she speaks through her poetry. Studying Akhmatova, I was struck by how much Lot's wife's circumstance speaks to every woman caught between the necessity for looking forward and the desire to remember.

Hagar and Ishmael

by Linda Kersh Steigman

Sarah saw the son, whom Hagar the Egyptian had borne to Abraham, playing. She said to Abraham, "Cast out that slavewoman and her son, for the son of that slave shall share the inheritance with my son Isaac." . . . Early the next morning Abraham took some bread and a skin of water, and gave them to Hagar. He placed them over her shoulder, together with the child, and sent her away. And she wandered about in the wilderness of Beer-Sheba. When the water was gone from the skin, she left the child under one of the bushes, and went and sat down at a distance, a bowshot away; for she thought, "Let me not look on as the child dies." And sitting thus afar, she burst into tears.

—Gen.21: 9, 14-16

Noonday sun beating down . . . merciless heat . . . my throat is parched . . . my body aches. I can go no farther. Numbness overcomes me. Cast out from my home of many years. Discarded. Despised.

Sarah, who brought me here from Egypt . . . Sarah, who gave me to Abraham to bear a child for him . . . my very presence enrages her.

And Abraham, with whom I lay and conceived that child, sent me out without warning. To perish in the desert?

Was I needed only to bear their child? Do I mean nothing to them after all these years of devotion and labor? How can they toss me out?

Replaced by a child . . . Sarah's child. What about Ishmael? Does not Abraham love Ishmael? How can a father abandon his child?

I can't bear to look at my son . . . lying pitifully under that bush . . . thirsty, scared. When we left the tent he was bewildered. Sarah and Isaac were nowhere to be seen, and Abraham wouldn't look at the lad, let alone talk to him.

I could see it in Ishmael's eyes . . . confusion, hurt. He asked me where we were going. "On a journey," I answered. Somehow he knew not to ask more. Yet he kept on glancing back at the tent, as if he expected his father to call after him, to call us back.

We walked in the hot sun. "Who will play with Isaac, my brother?" he asked. "Who will teach him to use the bow and arrow? Sarah and my father are old. Isaac needs me." Left unsaid were the words, "I need them."

I couldn't answer him for fear of giving in to my own terror. I need Abraham as much as Ishmael does. Being on my own petrifies me. Who will shelter me? Who will protect me? How can I comfort Ishmael when I feel so helpless myself?

There he lies . . . growing weaker by the moment. I fear that my cries frighten him. Yet he keeps on calling, "*Avi* . . . *Avi* . . ."

Who will hear us?

AUTHOR'S NOTE

In the summer of 1990, I had the good fortune to attend a *kallah,* sponsored by the Union of American Hebrew Congregations–Central Conference of American Rabbis Commission on Religious Living, at Brandeis University. I studied *midrash* with Dr. Norman Cohen, Dean of the New York School of Hebrew Union College–Jewish Institute of Religion. "Hagar and Ishmael" was the result of an additional session with Dr. Cohen on learning to write modern *midrash,* and was written in response to Genesis 21: 9-21.

I think the appeal of Hagar is universal. These lines speak to every woman ever abandoned by a spouse or lover; they evoke the terror felt by a woman, and the pain and fear for her children. Many women in the Torah are abandoned, either physically or emotionally, by significant men in their lives; Hagar represents but one of them.

Lech Lecha:
Sarah's Refrain

by Marla J. Feldman

God said: "Take your son, your favored one, Isaac, whom you love, and go . . . "

—Gen. 22:2

Lech lecha, lech lecha lech lecha lech lecha . . . the words reverberate in my brain like a mantra, repeating over and over and hovering at the edge of my consciousness as I grasp for a flicker of understanding. I wait at the window and watch . . . seeing nothing, seeing everything, searching in vain for the figures I know will not return.

Once before It called Abram. When he heard the command, *"Lech lecha,"* he obeyed. He followed The Voice. He passed the test. He walked from one life into another. He left his family to raise a family. He left his home for the promise of a homeland. All the while he assured me it was The Voice that commanded him. The Will that we should risk all. He promised I would understand one day. That I would be grateful for the journey. That I, too, would hear The Voice. *Lech lecha lech lecha lech lecha*

Eventually, I did hear It. Strange, amusing, unbelievable. In that moment I understood The Will and I was grateful for the long, torturous road that brought us to this place. My prayers were answered! A new life created! *Lech lecha lech lecha lech lecha*

But now, Abraham's journey continues and I am alone here. I miss even Hagar, my friend-turned-nemesis. I rejoiced when she left . . . yet now I find myself thinking of her, remembering how she faded away in the distance, my husband's child clinging to her side. I wonder . . . was she grateful for the journey? Did she ever

hear The Voice? Did she come to know the meaning of life or existence or suffering? Is she too lonely? *Lech lecha lech lecha lech lecha*
Now Abraham claims to hear The Voice once again. "*Lech lecha*," It commands. And he must take my son, my only son, whom I love, take Isaac to a place I do not know. Abraham says I cannot come with him on this journey. Am I being punished for banishing Hagar, I wonder? *Lech lecha lech lecha lech lecha* He says I have not been called. But neither was I called when The Voice led us from Ur to this place. Or to Egypt. Or Sodom. Or Gerar. Why, after all these years of sharing the journey must I stay behind? What makes the road we travel different this time? *Lech lecha lech lecha lech lecha* I can't get this refrain out of my mind . . . a thought is trying to focus, but I can't quite grasp It's meaning. *Lech lecha lech lecha lech lecha* I know I do not want to stay here alone. I want to go with them, protect them. *Lech lecha lech lecha lech lecha* I beg Abraham, please, take me with you! *Lech lecha lech lecha lech lecha* Don't leave me. *Lech lecha lech lecha lech lecha* Don't take my child. *Lech lecha lech lecha lech lecha* My child! Oh God! Don't take my child! *Lech lecha lech lecha lech lecha* I beg You! Please! Don't take my child! *Lech lecha lech lecha lech lecha* Don't take my child! *Lech lecha lech lecha lech lecha* Don't take my child! *Lech lecha lech lecha lech lecha Don't take my child Lech lecha lech lecha lech lecha Don't take my child lech lecha lech lecha lech lecha lech lech Don't take my child lech lecha lech lecha lech lecha Don't take my child Don't take my child Don't take my child Don't take my child Don't take my child Don't take my child Don't take my child Don't take my child Don't take my child Don't take my child.*

ADDITIONAL REFERENCES

The Lord said to Abram, "Go forth (*Lech Lecha*) from your native land and from your father's house to the land that I will show you."—Gen.12:1
The Lord appeared to [Abraham] by the terebinths of Mamre . . . Then one said,". . . your wife Sarah shall have a son." Sarah was listening at the entrance of the tent, which

was behind him . . . And Sarah laughed to herself . . . —Gen.
18:1-15

. . . Abraham took some bread and a skin of water, and
gave them to Hagar. He placed them over her shoulder, together with the child, and sent her away. And she wandered
about in the wilderness of Beer-sheba.—Gen. 21:14

AUTHOR'S NOTE

The phrase *lech lecha* is associated with the Torah portion in
which God commands Abraham to leave his home and go to
an unknown place to await his destiny. It is with the same
phrase that God commands Abraham to sacrifice Sarah's only
child, Isaac. In "Lech Lecha: *Sarah's Refrain,*" I imagine what
Sarah felt as she watched her destiny fade into the distance,
those same words resonating in her mind, *lech lecha* . . . This
midrash was inspired by a serigraph, based on the biblical text,
created by Pamela Feldman-Hill, in which the words *lech lecha*
float across the image.

Toward the Land of Moriah

by Mark Solomon

And [God] said: "Take now thy son, thine only son, whom thou lovest, even Isaac, and get thee into the land of Moriah; and offer him there for a burnt-offering upon one of the mountains which I will tell thee of."

   On the third day Abraham lifted up his eyes, and saw the place afar off.

—Gen. 22:2, 4

I lift my eyes,
see The Place, far off.

God asked for my son.
"Offer him," is how He put it.
"Please."

———

He didn't say, "Sacrifice."

———

It is not my son He wants.
It is my offering.

Not my son's life.

———

Mine.

AUTHOR'S NOTE

In January of 1991, I pleaded in vain with my son in Israel to come home from the *yeshivah* during the Scud attacks. Learning Torah in Jerusalem, he argued, was the proper response to

Hussein, to Haman, to Ameleik. He was anxious in the sealed room, with a gas-mask at his feet, but felt perfectly safe while he was studying.

"Come back then for the sake of your mother and your grand-mother."

"Are you asking me or are your commanding me?" I didn't know.

Encountering the *Akeidah* in the morning *davening* the next day, I marvelled at my son's *emunah* and wondered what was being asked or commanded of me.

(This poem is re-printed with permission of *Snake Nation Review* in which it first appeared in Issue No. 9, 1994.)

Letter from Isaac

by Linda Kersh Steigman

And Sarah died in Kiriath-arba—now Hebron—in the land of Canaan.

—Gen. 23:2

Dear Ishmael,

I hope that this letter finds you and Hagar in good health. I wanted you to know that I just received news of my mother's death. She has been buried in the cave at Machpelah. My feelings are so confused . . . Since the incident on Mount Moriah I have had no contact with either Mother or Father. Father knows where I am, but has made no effort to contact me until sending his servant Eleazar with this news about Mother.

I've been thinking about my parents. What do I really know about their relationship? What does any child know? They met in Ur, married, and then moved with Grandfather Terah and cousin Lot to Haran. My parents left Haran after Grandfather Terah died, when Father heard God tell him to leave his home and move to a place that God would show him. I wonder what else Father heard that convinced him to leave Haran without knowing where he was going? And how much of this did he share with Mother?

For many years after that they led a semi-nomadic existence. The frequent moves must have been difficult on both Mother and Father, and on their marriage. They were always leaving familiar surroundings and people that they had grown to love.

Over the years my mother dropped hints, some not so subtle, that Father was frequently preoccupied with having children and grandchildren. In his sleep he would mutter, "I will make of you a great nation . . ." "I will make you exceedingly numerous." My mother felt terrible. Did Father blame her for not having children?

Was that why, after many years, she suggested that your mother bear a son . . . you, Ishmael . . . for our Father?

Once, early in their marriage, when they went down to Egypt because of the famine . . . that's where our mothers met . . . and again, many years later in Gerar, Father told people that my mother was his sister, not his wife. My mother went along with this charade, but it was so confusing and frightening to her. He said it was for her protection, but somehow she didn't feel very safe being away from him.

Even though I was very young when you left, I remember Mother and Father arguing over you and your mother. When I asked where you were, they said you had gone away. "When are they coming back?" I remember asking. There was no answer. In later years I pressed Father on this. Although he would never answer me directly, he implied that your leaving was my mother's wish, not his.

I can't imagine how shocked they were to learn that my mother would become pregnant so late in life. It's hard to believe that Father was one hundred years old when I was born.

I now realize that I grew up coddled by my mother, and that both of my parents had great expectations of me. My mother wanted me to be the one to inherit all of my father's wealth . . . I think that's part of the reason you and Hagar had to leave. And Father? Father kept on talking about his relationship with God, and how it was up to me to carry on this relationship, this Covenant, after he died.

That's what makes the whole frightening incident at Mt. Moriah so confusing. I remember it as if it were just yesterday.

Father woke me early in the morning, and told me to get ready for a journey. My mother was still in her tent, asleep. The donkeys were already saddled, and the two servants who would accompany us were waiting with food, water, and wood.

Just as we were leaving the compound, in such a rush that I didn't have a chance to ask why or where, my mother came out of her tent. For some reason she didn't call after us. She didn't ask where we were going, just sadly waved goodbye. This is my last memory of her.

We left Beer Sheba just as the sun was rising. We rode north, towards Moriah. When we had gone to Moriah before, it had taken us less than a day. But this time the journey seemed to take forever. Usually on our journeys together Father would be very talkative, but on this journey he seemed off in a world by himself.

It wasn't until the third day after we left Beer Sheba that Father looked up at a mountain and said "We're here." The servants unloaded the wood, and I realized that we were going to climb to the top of the mountain to offer a sacrifice. When I asked Father about the lamb for the sacrifice, his words were . . . and I vividly remember them . . . "God will see to the sheep for His burnt offering, my son." I remember thinking that he was in a trance, unreachable by me or by anyone else. But all my life I had trusted him. I had no reason to stop now.

What happened . . . or almost happened . . . on top of that mountain was so awful. It still gives me nightmares. When Father released me, to sacrifice the ram instead, all I remember is running down the mountain and away from him as fast as I could. I kept running until the full impact of what almost happened hit me. I remember collapsing in sobs and falling asleep, only to continue running when I awoke.

I have seen neither Father nor Mother since that time. Even now, receiving word of her death, I wonder what my mother knew when she saw us riding off early that morning. It was unlike her not to ask where we were going. She must have known that something out of the ordinary was going to happen.

In a way, I grieved for my parents after Mt. Moriah. It's hard to explain, but I think that they ceased to be my parents when I could no longer trust them to keep me safe from harm.

Eleazar tells me that Father has asked him to find a bride for me from among Father's kinfolk in Haran. I didn't think Father cared whom I married. But if I had thought about it, I would have realized that it is my responsibility, despite this estrangement, to transmit the covenant "from generation to generation."

I miss you, Ishmael.

Love,

Isaac.

AUTHOR'S NOTE

When invited to be a *Shabbat* speaker on Outreach, I prefer to deliver my remarks as a *dvar* Torah. On this particular Shabbat (Chaye Sarah) my focus was parents whose adult children had intermarried.

Families who face this issue exhibit many of the same dynamics as biblical families. What could be a better place to start than with our first Jewish family . . . Abraham, Sarah, and Isaac. In the Torah, we don't hear Isaac's voice; in families facing intermarriage, the (adult) child's voice is seldom heard. Isaac's memories and observations about his family give our families an additional way of looking at themselves.

Sarah's Sacrifice

by Margaret Kaufman

And the life of Sarah was a hundred and seven and twenty
years; these were the years of the life of Sarah.
—Gen.23: 1

I think of it so much, I mean the time
when I was told I'd bear a child—me,
past my time—far more than past—old.
When I was told, I laughed. Later,
there was that between us: I had laughed.

You could say then from the outset we were split,
levity between us like a ridge,
a place where one could climb or fall.
I loved my husband, but Abraham
was filled with thought, his head
heavy as the date palm's leafy crest,
one ear bent always toward the sky.
Some laughter would have served him well.

One God—so be it.
It wasn't that I didn't hold with him. Only
it was my lot to see to the tents, water jars,
tethers, a mother goat bleating for her stray,
all the shaggy herd, the other women,
where they would stay when we pitched camp.

I was old, fragile in belief.
For giving us a son, we thanked this God;
because I'd laughed we called him Isaac.

Who can say what laughter means?
Is it another name for doubt? Delight?
As when you watch a seed knife through the earth,
its light green sheath
whittle dirt to light, so I admired
each limb, each ear, toes,
each of Isaac's hands. Abraham
grew more intense, his joy translated into fervor,
Isaac a test: Ishmael teased him, Hagar looked aside—
it shames me that I sent them both away, saying
"Let your God take care of them."
He did, and then moved on to me.

Now, when I stare into the night,
watch the moon's cold light
pare the edges of palm fronds white and sharp,
I see with Isaac's eyes that raised up knife.
Did everything he knew then fall away?
Did he cry out? When I remember Isaac *then,*
my tongue dries like the husks of date fronds,
it rustles words, my arms flail
like grass blown down, my spirit shreds.

"Who made me see the ram?" he asks.
We speak long in the evenings, Abraham
stirring the fire with sticks, watching embers
fly up toward the stars, bright bits
like living creatures rising into the dark.
My stick starts nothing, stirs rubble,
ash heaped on ash, as after the burnt offering
very little's left, bone shard, knuckle
of the lamb or goat, whatever it was
we sacrificed for God.

AUTHOR'S NOTE

I wrote this poem because it seemed remarkable that Sarah drops out of the narrative at its most important moment. I wanted to explore what her thoughts would have been and the connection between laughter and belief.

The poem was first published by the Gefn Press in London in a limited edition. It has also been set as a cantata by Ben Steinberg, the noted Canadian composer.

Isaac and Ishmael

by Philip Cohen

*Then Abraham gave up the ghost and died in a good old age,
an old man, and full of years and was gathered to his people.
And his sons Isaac and Ishmael buried him in the cave of
Machpelah in the field of Ephron the son of Zohar the Hittite,
which is before Mamre.*

—Gen.25:8-9

Much has been written over the years about Isaac and Ishmael, two
half brothers who shared the same father. The stories of their
respective labors, and their results, have been told more times
than anyone would care to count. Our world owes much to them.

But back then, when the world was still young, before the Age
of Enlightenment and automatic weapons, Isaac and Ishmael
were just two guys with only the vaguest sense of mission and no
sense of the enormity that would be wrought on their account by
their descendants. Back then they were just two guys living out
their lives in the desert, trying to get from day to day, trying to
work free of their respective ghosts, trying to figure out what they
wanted to be. Judaism and Islam were not on their minds.

It is not known where Ishmael was hanging his hat on the day
he received word his father had died. But the news obviously
travelled fast, because he was at his half brother's side when the
old man was laid to rest in the Cave of Machpelah.

This cave, as you may already know, was the place that
Abraham purchased not long before, on the occasion of the pass-
ing of his wife Sarah, as a burial place for her. It was the first piece
of property Abraham had ever truly owned, being nomadic by
profession. He bought the cave from a Hittite called Ephron ben
Zohar for four hundred pieces of silver, about three times its actual

value. That he was taken didn't matter. For here Abraham could lay his wife down to rest, and here he could now lie beside her—lifeless, shrouded, eyes shut, waxen, the future now decidedly left to others.

For years Ishmael swore to anyone with the time to listen that he was through with Abraham. His father had banished him and, worse, had banished his mother, Hagar, to the desert. There, mother and son would have dried up like tumbleweeds and blown away were it not for divine intervention. Because of Abraham's act, Ishmael carried within him an anger whose end he was never able to reach, though he traveled long and hard down its dark passages. He lived out his youth with a mother but without a father. He never wanted to see his father again, dead or alive.

Yet when he heard about his father's death, a power within him overcame the urge only to hate Abraham. The anger did not evaporate; instead, he saw that there was more to his feelings toward his father than anger alone. In the midst of the memories of his banishment, there appeared now for the first time ever an image, a fleeting image but tactile and real nonetheless. Through this image Ishmael recalled feeling a strong and reassuring hand on his left shoulder and hearing words tinged with sadness: "God will be with you."

Ishmael knew in an instant, and without doubt, that he had to return to Canaan to pay his last respects to Abraham. He left with utmost dispatch, not thinking of anything but his father—certainly not thinking of Isaac, who would undoubtedly be there, not thinking of this half brother whom he once mocked in a fit of adolescent jealousy but whom he never knew really, and who shared with him the same father.

He arrived at the Cave of Machpelah just as Isaac and Rebecca came with a small procession and with the wagon bearing Abraham's shrouded corpse.

Though it had been some decades since Ishmael and Isaac had seen one another, the two half brothers recognized each other immediately. The circumstances under which they were meeting facilitated their recognition. But more than that, the fraternal bond they shared informed the knowledge that facing one was the other's brother. Even if they had been in a distant city and encountered one another by chance in a crowded marketplace, their recognition would have been as instantaneous as it was here at their father's grave.

They nodded to each other, grudgingly to all outward appearances. Yet beneath superficial appearances there was a stirring both men felt and neither understood. This was their feelings toward one another rising involuntarily and inchoately. I do not speak here of hatred. On the contrary, I speak of a kind of love that had never had the opportunity to develop, that was nonetheless real, and that had lain dormant beneath the burden of the years. Face to face contact aroused this emotion and brought their feelings for one another back to life, if only faintly.

Neither would have predicted this stirring within them, had they the capacity to think about such matters. Yet both intuitively recognized what was going on as it happened. It was the stirring of blood, the awakening of connection that defies language, that two brothers—even two half brothers, sons of Abraham—felt when fate drew them together after an absence of years.

In response to their emotional reaction, without thinking, each extended a hand to the other; the handshake became a clumsily executed hug. Then they pulled away from each other without speaking a word and, either embarrassed or surprised, turned quickly away—ostensibly to attend to the business at hand.

Without exchanging a word, the two carried Abraham into the cave and gently placed him beside Sarah's shrouded body.

They removed themselves from the cave, and stood at its opening, in silence, at the head of the small group. For many minutes no one knew what to say. There was at that time no tradition of funeral prayers. No *tsiduk ha-din,* no *el malei rahamim,* no *kaddish yatom.* These things had not yet been worked out. So instead they were mute.

A hot wind blew in from the desert, burning their cheeks and filling their eyes with dust.

Then Isaac spoke.

"We are here to say goodbye to my father, Abraham," he said, then hesitated, attempting to find the right words. "I loved my father, but he was no saint. He taught me and cared for me. When my mother died, he made certain that I had a wife . . .

"But there was that incident on Mount Moriah. I never understood what came over him. I've forgiven him for it," said Isaac, remembering momentarily the sacrificial knife poised at his throat and ready for the kill. "But," he added, "I'll never forget it, and I don't believe I'll ever understand it."

Isaac pulled his garment around him as the wind continued to blow. He went on:

"My father now lies next to my mother. It is fitting that they should be together in death. For together they led a life of richness and adventure. They came here as strangers from Haran to fulfill a mission both believed in. Both did what they could to make a home for me here, too, and for that I'll always be grateful. I know that someday I'll lie there beside them. But not now. Now we must carry on. For now we all must say goodbye to a man who was larger than life, but who also was flesh and blood, whose life gave life, and who made the future possible."

AAd with those concluding words, everyone assembled at the mouth of the cave turned around and walked away slowly, simultaneously, as if one mourning body. Ishmael and Isaac pulled the wagon.

Thus Ishmael and Isaac found themselves walking next to each other back to Isaac's home. Through their shared burden, they felt a common bond touching them. There was inexplicable comfort in this silence.

Later, outside Isaac's tent, over a small meal of vegetables and bread, they spoke to each other for the first time in years.

"Isaac," said Ishmael. "Today has been a revelation. I came to say farewell to my father. That alone was hard. I don't expect you'd understand how hard. But . . ." he shifted uncomfortably, reaching for words he was uncertain he could find. "But . . . but meeting you, seeing you again, and hearing your words at the burial site . . ." Ishmael trailed off, and reached for a piece of bread, unable to continue.

"I never expected you'd come," said Isaac. "I'm glad you did. You were most welcome there this afternoon. But I confess I was surprised seeing you at the cave."

Ishmael said, "I had to come. I had no choice."

Isaac hesitated a moment, then continued. "You know, he often spoke of you, especially after Sarah died."

Ishmael brightened. "What did he say about me?"

"He said he'd always had regrets about expelling you. He wondered how you were getting on. Sure, we'd hear word of you from time to time. We knew, in fact, that you were getting on well enough. He drank a toast to you when he heard about your marriage."

Ishmael smiled. It was small comfort that his father had heard of his taking an Egyptian wife, but it was better than the nothing he thought he'd had.

Isaac continued, "So when Father would say he wondered about you, I came to understand that he meant he wanted to know more than what traders carry as gossip. I believe he would have loved a visit from you." There was a touch of accusation in Isaac's voice.

Ishmael felt some of the old anger welling inside his stomach. He said, "That was something I would have never been able to do. He would have had to send for me or come and find me. I wasn't that far away; in fact I knew that he knew what city I was living in. He was the one who gave me the boot, brother, not the other way around."

Both men stared into the distance seeking an invisible spot on the horizon.

Ishmael said, "I have to say that I was surprised at what you said today. I would have expected you to say something more complimentary about our father. After all, you were the one who got to stay. Instead you were ambivalent.

"What happened at Mount Moriah?"

"Ah yes, Mount Moriah. Well, sometime after you left . . ."

"You mean, after I was invited to leave," said Ishmael.

"Yes, after you were told to go," said Isaac. "He woke me one morning. 'We're taking a trip,' he said. 'Where to?' I asked him. He didn't answer. So I got up, got dressed, and we went for a walk in the desert for over two days—me, him, two servants and a couple of donkeys."

"Just like that you went for a walk?"

"Yeah. It was strange, walking all that time. The old man never said a word the whole trip. He had this look of determination in his eyes, like he was overcome by some outside force. He was very grim. Finally we got to the foot of Mount Moriah. There he broke his silence. He told the two servants to stay put, that he and I were going to climb the mountain to make a sacrifice. Me he told to carry the wood we'd brought for the sacrificial fire and to follow him up the mountain."

"Did he tell you why he was interested in making a sacrifice at that particular spot?"

"No. Not at all. Suddenly he stopped the procession and we went up the mountain. All he told me was that God would provide the lamb for the offering. It made good sense to me at the moment. Of course what he said and what he meant were two entirely different things."

"What happened?"

"What happened was we got to the top of the mountain and he assembled a small altar. So far, so good. But then he threw me on it. He literally threw me on this pile of wood, and I lay there. I was dazed. I couldn't figure out what was going on. My father had just pushed me on top of a woodpile intended for a lamb. I just lay there waiting to see what would happen next."

"And what did happen?"

"He came at me with the sacrificial knife we had brought. A knife so sharp that if he had just touched my throat with it—which is where he seemed to be heading with it—I would have bled to death. About that I have no doubt. His eyes were barely open as he lifted the knife high enough to give him some leverage. Then, just as he had begun to bring it down, he stopped."

Ishmael exhaled; he looked in Isaac's eyes and was startled. For a moment he thought he was looking in a mirror. Not the facial features exactly, just the eyes. But the eyes were enough. For in the telling, Isaac had taken on a haunted look that emanated from the eyes. And although Ishmael had never actually seen it in himself, he had felt it a hundred times.

And then Ishmael knew that on that day he not only buried his father, but found his brother, a comrade. And although relations between the two over subsequent years were never to be easy, they were never impossibly difficult, either.

AUTHOR'S NOTE

I chose to write this *midrash* partly because of the question it explicitly asks, and partly out of the question it implicitly asks. I have always been surprised by Ishmael's appearance at the burial of his father. That, of course, is the point of departure for the *midrash.* But the deeper and hence more interesting question is about the individual identities of Ishmael and Isaac and their relationship with each other. This is a question not only of two biblical figures, but also of the issue of what each man symbolizes.

The Dream of Isaac

Howard Schwartz

When the time to give birth was at hand, there were twins in her [Rebecca's] womb. The first one emerged red, like a hairy mantle all over; so they named him Esau. Then his brother emerged, holding on to the heel of Esau; so they named him Jacob.

—Gen. 25:24

It is said that as he grew older Isaac put the journey to Mount Moriah out of his mind. Even to Rebecca, his wife, he would not speak of what had happened. So circumspect did he become, that by the time of his marriage at the age of forty no one could remember the last time he had spoken on the subject. So it seems likely that during the period in which his wife was expecting a child the old memory came to his mind even less often, for Rebecca had grown ripe with her waiting, which was already much longer than the old wives had estimated.

On one such night, while he and Rebecca were sleeping side by side, Isaac dreamed for the first time of the sacrifice that had taken place almost thirty years before. But this dream was even more real than the actual incident, for then his confusion had saved him from his fear; now, all the terror he had not noticed was with him. A faceless man chained him to a great rock and held a knife against his neck. He felt the blade poised to press down when the sun emerging from behind a cloud blinded them both. At the same time, they heard the frantic honking of a goose whose gray and white feathers had become entangled in the thorns of a nearby bush. It was then that the fierce and silent man, whom Isaac now saw was his father, put down the blade and pulled the bird free from the thorns and berries. As he brought it back, Isaac saw how it struggled in his hands. Then, when the goose was pressed firmly to the rock, Isaac watched as his father pulled back the white throat and drew the blade. He saw especially how white was the neck and how cleanly the blade cut through. At last Abraham put down the blade and unbound his son and they embraced. It was then that Isaac opened his eyes, felt the arms of his wife as she tried to wake him, and heard her whispering that the child was about to be born.

When Isaac understood he sat up in bed and hurried from the room to wake the midwife, who had been living with them for almost three weeks. Two hours later Rebecca gave birth, first to one son and then to another. The first was hairy, his skin red; the second came forth with his hand on his brother's heel. Isaac found himself fascinated as he watched the midwife wash the infants in warm water. The first son, whom they came to call Esau, was born with an umbilical cord that was dark purple, the color of blood. But his second son, whose name became Jacob, had a cord that was soft and white as pure wax. It was this perfectly woven rope that Isaac found most intriguing, for reasons he could not comprehend. And he sensed a strange terror as he unsheathed a knife and drew the blade to sever this last link between what was and what would be. For it was then the dream of that night came back to him, and he saw in the same instant how the hands of his father had held down the goose, and how the sharp blade had cut across its neck, soft and white, like the severed cord he held in his own hands.

ADDITIONAL REFERENCES

And Abraham stretched forth his hand, and took the knife to slay his son.—Gen.22:10

When Abraham looked up, his eye fell upon a ram, caught in the thicket by its horns. So Abraham went and took the ram and offered it up as a burnt offering in place of his son.—Gen.22:13

AUTHOR'S NOTE

This tale offers an extreme example of the midrashic method. Just as one late *midrash* states that Abraham *did* slay Isaac, whose soul then ascended on high, so here the ram caught in the bush (Gen.22:13) has been replaced with a goose. This takes place in a dream attributed to Isaac, thirty years after the *Akeidah.* And in dreams, as we know, events are transformed. The purpose of substituting the goose for the ram is to link the sacrifice of the goose with the cutting of the umbilical cords of Esau and Jacob. The effect is to link the two episodes, a common midrashic device, and to imply a link between the sacrifice that saves the son and the cutting of the cord that is necessary for the child to live. The notion that the cord of Esau is blood-red is deduced from the description of Esau at his birth, when he emerged red all over (Gen.25:25). The pure white of Jacob's cord symbolizes the purity that Jacob is considered to represent in the *aggadah,* despite his frequent use of trickery (Gen.27:5; 30:35-43).

All Prophecies Fulfilled

by David A. Katz

So Isaac sent for Jacob and blessed him. He instructed him, saying, "You shall not take a wife from among the Canaanite women. Up, go to Paddan-aram, to the house of Bethuel, your mother's father, and take a wife there from among the daughters of Laban, your mother's brother. May El Shaddai bless you, make you fertile and numerous, so that you become an assembly of peoples. May He grant the blessing of Abraham to you and your offspring, that you may possess the land where you are sojourning, which God gave to Abraham.

—Gen. 28:1-4

Isaac and Rebecca lay next to each other in bed. They did not speak. That day their first born son, Esau had married Judith and Basemath. They were now his wives and neither of them was Jewish. So the marriages were a source of great bitterness to Isaac and Rebecca.

Rebecca turned to Isaac. Her voice was ice. "How *could* he? How could he do this to us?" But Isaac did not even hear the words of his wife because of the sadness and anger that had overtaken him.

When Rebecca saw that Isaac did not answer she turned in frustration and lay on her back. She could not tolerate the thought of Isaac giving his blessing to Esau. How could Esau's women hope to play the parts of her daughters-in-law? How could they expect that she would accept them? Who did they think they were? She needed a plan that would see to it that the blessing went to Jacob.

She glanced over at Isaac. His eyes were closed and she saw how innocent he was. Her plan would have to protect his good name. She closed her eyes and thought hard. Suddenly an idea came to her—and in the darkness Rebecca smiled.

Now Isaac's eyes were closed but he was not asleep. He was thinking about the covenantal blessing of land and seed, how God had spoken to him when he was alone, saying, "I will be with you and bless you; I will give all these lands to you and to your offspring, fulfilling the oath that I swore to your father Abraham. I will make your descendants as numerous as the stars of heaven." And he now asked himself, "How could Esau inherit the land if his seed were from Hittite women?" He needed a plan to see to it that the covenantal blessing went to Jacob. He opened his eyes and turned to his beloved wife, Rebecca. He could barely see the outline of her body for his eyes were weak in his old age. But Rebecca appeared to be asleep. How innocent she was. Whatever plan he devised could not involve her. Her name would have to be clear and her reputation unharmed. Suddenly, an idea came to him—and in the darkness Isaac smiled.

The next morning Isaac sent for Esau and said to him, "My son." And he answered, "Here I am." And Isaac said, "I am old now and I do not know how soon I will die. Take your gear, your quiver and your bow, and go out into the open and hunt me some game. Then prepare a dish for me such as I like, and bring it to me to eat, so that I may give you my innermost blessing before I die."

Esau was eager for the blessing and after waiting patiently for Isaac to complete his instructions, quickly turned to leave the tent.

How simple it was to get Esau out of the encampment and into the field, Isaac thought. He so loved the outdoors. He would be gone for hours, first hunting the game then preparing the meal, plenty of time for Isaac to call Jacob into his tent to explain his thoughts and feelings to him, then secretly to bestow upon him the covenantal blessing.

Now Rebecca had stood at the opening of the tent, listening to every word Isaac told Esau. Seeing her chance to execute her own plan she ran to Jacob and said, "I overheard your father speaking to your brother Esau, saying, "Bring me some game and prepare a dish for me to eat, that I may bless you, with the LORD's approval, before I die." Now, my son, listen carefully as I instruct you. Go to the flock and fetch me two choice kids, and I will make of them a dish for your father, such as he likes. Then take it to your father to eat, in order that he may bless you before he dies."

But Jacob was afraid and answered his mother, "But my brother Esau is a hairy man and I am smooth-skinned. If my father touches me, I shall appear to him as a trickster and bring upon myself a curse, not a blessing." But his mother said to him, "Your curse, my son, be upon me! Just do as I say and go fetch them for me."

Then Rebecca quickly prepared Isaac's favorite dish, took Esau's best clothes out of his tent and dressed Jacob in them. Then she covered his hands and the hairless part of his neck with the skins of kids. She put in the hands of her son Jacob the dish and the bread she had prepared. And then she returned to her tent.

Jacob went to his father and said, "Father." And he said, "Yes, which of my sons are you?" Jacob said to his father, "I am Esau, your first-born; I have done as you told me. Pray sit up and eat of my game, that you may give me your innermost blessing." Isaac said to his son, "What is this?! You have been so quick to find it my son!" And he said, "Because the Lord your God granted my good fortune."

Isaac was confused. Which son stood before him now? If it were Jacob, he could give the blessing to him immediately. But if it were Esau, he would have to find some excuse to postpone the blessing.

Isaac said to Jacob, "Come closer that I may feel you, my son— whether you are really my son Esau or not." So Jacob drew close to his father Isaac, who felt him and wondered, "The voice is the voice of Jacob, yet the hands are the hands of Esau."

Then one last time Isaac tried to find out which son stood before him. He asked, "Are you really my son Esau?" And when Jacob said, "I am," Isaac said, "Serve me and let me eat of my son's game that I may give you my innermost blessing." So Jacob served him and he ate. And Jacob brought him wine and he drank. Then his father Isaac said to him, "Come close and kiss me, my son." So Jacob went up and kissed him. When Jacob leaned over, Isaac smelled his clothes but still could not tell whether it was Esau or Jacob who stood before him. What could he do? Unless he knew that it was Jacob who stood before him he could not bestow the blessing.

Then Isaac thought, "Neither son has ever heard the content of the covenantal blessing. What do they know of promises of land or seed? Neither had been there when Abraham was blessed or when he himself had received the blessings from heaven. So Isaac turned his face to the son who stood before him and he lifted his hands and he said:

> "May God give you
> of the dew of heaven and the fat of the earth,
> Abundance of new grain and wine.
> Let peoples serve you,
> And nations bow to you;
> Be master over your brothers,
> And let your mother's sons bow to you.
> Cursed be they who curse you,
> Blessed they who bless you."

So Isaac never mentioned the holy land or the promise of descendants. He spoke only about the dew of heaven and the fat of the earth. It made no difference to him who would bow to whom.

No sooner had Jacob left the presence of his father—after Isaac had finished blessing Jacob—than his brother Esau came back from his hunt. He too prepared a dish and brought it to his father. And he said to his father, "Let my father sit up and eat of his son's game, so that you may give me your innermost blessing." His father Isaac said to him, "Who are you?" And he said, "I am your son Esau, your first-born!" Isaac said, "Draw close," and he smelled the field on Esau's clothes and he felt his hands.

Now Isaac knew the truth.

Surely, this *was* Esau and it had been Jacob who had come before to steal the blessing of his brother. Isaac knew what he had to do. He made his body tremble. He made his voice shake. And he made himself appear the victim. "Who was it then," he demanded, "that hunted game and brought it to me? Moreover, I ate of it before you came, and I blessed him; now he must remain blessed!" When Esau heard his father's words, he burst into wild and bitter sobbing, and said to this father, "Bless me too, Father!" But he answered, "Your brother came with guile and took away your blessing." Esau said, "Was he, then, named Jacob that he might supplant me these two times? First he took away my birthright and now he has taken away my blessing!" And he added, "Have you not reserved a blessing for me?" Isaac answered, saying to Esau, "But I have made him master over you: I have given him all his brothers for servants, and sustained him with grain and wine. What, then can I still do for you, my son?" And Esau said to his father, "Have you but one blessing, Father? Bless me too, Father!" and Esau wept aloud. And his father Isaac answered, saying to him,

> "See, your abode shall enjoy the fat of the earth
> And the dew of heaven above.
> Yet by your sword you shall live,
> And you shall serve your brother;
> But when you grow restive,
> You shall break his yoke from your neck."

So once again, Isaac did not speak of land or seed. He did not bestow the covenantal blessing on Esau for Esau had married Hittite women.

Now Esau harbored a grudge against Jacob because of the blessing which his father had given him, and Esau said to himself, "Let but the mourning period of my father come, and I will kill my brother Jacob." When the words of her older son Esau were reported to Rebecca, she became very upset. Surely Esau would confront Jacob and Jacob would try to save himself by telling Esau what she had done.

So she sent for Jacob and said to him, "Your brother Esau is consoling himself by planning to kill you. Now, my son, listen to me. Flee at once to Haran, to my brother Laban. Stay with him a while, until your brother's fury subsides—until your brother's anger against you subsides—and he forgets what you have done to him. Then I will fetch you from there. Let me not lose you both in one day!" Tomorrow your father will instruct you."

That night Isaac and Rebecca lay next to each other in bed. They did not speak; they were both very worried.

Isaac thought to himself, surely Jacob and Esau will compare their blessings. Rebecca will hear it all and she will discover that neither one received the covenantal promise. Then she will know that I deceived my sons and her as well. I must send Jacob away. But what reason should I give to Rebecca for sending him off?

As Isaac lay still, Rebecca's mind was racing. If she were to tell Isaac that Esau was planning to kill Jacob, Isaac would attempt to reconcile the brothers. Jacob would surely tell his father how she had managed the deception. She had to find a reason to send Jacob away.

Rebecca said to Isaac "I am disgusted with my life because of the Hittite women. If Jacob marries a Hittite woman like these, from among the native women, what good will life be to me?"

Isaac sighed with relief. Here was his reason to send Jacob away. Jacob must go to Rebecca's family, far away from the Hittite women. Isaac turned to Rebecca and said, "Then we must send him to your family in Paddan-aram to find a wife. Tomorrow he shall go."

In the darkness, Rebecca smiled. She did not see the smile on Isaac's face as he turned to go to sleep.

The next morning Isaac sent for Jacob and Jacob came into Isaac's tent. Now the moment had come. "Draw close to me," said Isaac. And Jacob drew close. Then Isaac instructed him, saying, "You shall not take a wife from among the Canaanite women. Up, go to Paddan-aram, to the house of Bethuel, your mother's father, and take a wife there from among the daughters of Laban, your mother's brother."

Isaac placed his hands on Jacob's head and spoke the words that were the promises from heaven. "May El Shaddai bless you, make you fertile and numerous, so that you become an assembly of peoples. May He grant the blessing of Abraham to you and your offspring, that you may possess the land where you are sojourning, which God gave to Abraham."

Esau stood outside the tent as Isaac spoke to Jacob and when he overheard Isaac speak, he thought, surely this was the blessing my brother stole and now as he is sent away, my father Isaac, repeats it once again. When Esau saw that Isaac had blessed Jacob and sent him off to Paddan-aram to take a wife from there, charging him, as he blessed him, "You shall not take a wife from among Canaanite women," and that Jacob would obey his father and mother and go to Paddan-aram, Esau realized that the Cana-anite women displeased his father. He lowered his head. No, he would not pursue Jacob.

That evening at dinner, Jacob's place was empty. No one spoke to each other for the burden of events was carried in everyone's heart. Isaac only touched his food. Esau sat in silence while Judith and Basemath, his women, quietly helped Rebecca clear the table.

But Jacob, Jacob was journeying to a new place. The evening sky of the desert was filled with stars and the land upon which Jacob rested his head was holy. All prophecies had been fulfilled. Two nations had been in Rebecca's womb and the younger would serve the elder. And in the heavens God looked down upon the scene and smiled.

ADDITIONAL REFERENCES

Based on Genesis 26:34—28:9.

AUTHOR'S NOTE

In rabbinical school, I took a Bible class in which I learned that the covenantal blessing included both the promise of Israel and the promise of descendants. When I read the story of Jacob and Esau, it dawned upon me that Isaac does not give away this important blessing until *after* the great deception scene. What is going on? My midrash offers one theory.

Ignored Sons, Favorite Sons

by Adam Fisher

And Isaac sent away Jacob . . .

—Gen. 28:5

1. ISAAC

Mother ignored my tears,
told father, "Send Ishmael away."
But, he was my brother;
we played together.
Later, father took me to the mountain,
spoke tenderly, then distantly,
tied me down and took the knife.
I hid my terror,
dread of disobeying
horror of obeying.
He ignored my whimpering.
Afterwards he never noticed
I ran down the other side.
Did he care about my hurt,
that I could never speak to him again?
I remember all that now
and my vow, "I'll know my children."
But I could never talk to Esau,
I only loved the game he cooked;
never was close to Jacob,
he was so shy and scheming.
And now that I have just blessed him
instead of Esau,
heard Esau's pain,

I see I couldn't tell them apart,
didn't know them any more
than my father knew me.

2. JACOB

I liked being my mother's favorite,
but when she told me
"Trick father,
take the blessing from your brother,"
I was afraid he'd find me out.
Because of her, I won the blessing;
because of it, I had to flee.
Lonely at night,
I called to God;
then endured deception,
to marry Rachel,
promised myself
my sons would get along.
I remember my anguish
when they sent Joseph away.
He was my favorite—
gave him the colorful coat,
ignored my other sons.
Late at night
I ask myself,
"Did I do to him
what was done to me?"

ADDITIONAL REFERENCES

She said to Abraham, "Cast out that slave-woman and her son . . ."—Gen. 21.10
   And Abraham picked up the knife to slay his son. —Gen. 22.10

Then prepare a dish for me such as I like . . . so that I may give you my innermost blessing before I die.—Gen. 27.4

When Esau heard his father's words he burst into wild and bitter sobbing . . .—Gen. 27.34

Take it to your father to eat, in order that he may bless you before he dies.—Gen. 27.10

Jacob left Beer-sheba . . . stopped for the night . . . had a dream; a stairway . . .—Gen. 28.10-12

When morning came, there was Leah! So he said to Laban, . . . "Why did you deceive me?"—Gen. 29.35

Now Israel loved Joseph best of all his sons . . . and he made him an ornamented tunic.—Gen. 37.3

AUTHOR'S NOTE

The sparse nature of the biblical narrative leaves tantalizing spaces in which to fill in imaginative possibilities. I find this to be a process that involves me deeply in the text. I feel my way into the story so that I can wander through it and get inside the personalities. It is a deeply humanizing process because we become acquainted with and empathize with all their pain, perplexity and joy. It is a deeply spiritual process as well for it helps to reach the deepest places within us—the places from which we become aware of God's Presence.

The Rape of Dinah

by Barbara Sherrod

Now Dinah, the daughter whom Leah had borne to Jacob, went out to visit the daughters of the land. Shechem, son of Hamor the Hivite, chief of the country, saw her, and took her and lay with her by force. Being strongly drawn to Dinah and in love with the maiden, he spoke to her tenderly. So Shechem said to his father Hamor, "Get me this girl as a wife."

—Gen. 34:1-4

I went out to visit the Canaanite women, who listen and do not laugh when I complain of how it is to have only brothers, a mother weary with childbearing and a father always preoccupied. We played a game of question and answer as we washed the clothing in the stream. The women glanced up and saw Shechem, son of Hamor. He was looking steadfastly at me. I could see he was drunk for he weaved on his horse and hiccupped. There was a lazy smile in his eyes. All at once he rode into our midst, took me up and rode to his tent. He was large and heavy; whenever I struggled, he struck me in the face or breast.

In his tent he drank from his cup and asked me to drink as well. When I would not, he let fly the back of his hand, drawing blood from my nose. He drew out a knife with which he cut my cheek and tore my dress, saying that he would carve his mark upon my breast so that no other man would have me. Then, not minding the flow of blood, he threw himself on me and took me by force. As though from a great distance, I heard myself crying and moaning. I pushed at him with all my strength and scratched until his face bled, but the more I resisted, the more insistent he became, and he hurt me again and again until he was spent and fell into oblivion.

Seeing that he slept, I crawled into a corner. I wished to clean my wounds with the shreds of my garment, but fearing that the slightest movement might wake him, I remained still, shivering and feeling the blood dry on my cheeks and breast.

When he did wake and saw what he had done, he grew tearful with remorse. He berated and cursed himself for hurting me and blamed the drink. Believing it was possible that I could forgive him, I suppose, he swore he would make it up to me and vowed to marry me.

I said I would be his wife if he would first permit me to go home, and when at last I entered the tent of my father and saw him sitting, old and grim and alone, I told him what had happened. He was silent a very long time. My father is a man who takes every event in his children's lives as God's punishment on him; therefore, he said nothing about me but thought only of his own woe.

Weeping and angry, I ran out to the fields to tell my brothers. I wished to find Simeon and Levi, for I was their pet and they coddled and teased me and would not rebuke me for what had happened. But I soon wished I had never found them and never told them. Their fury was overpowering, and they pledged vengeance.

I begged them not to set their minds on retribution, knowing that if they repaid violence with slaughter, their lands would be taken from them and they would forfeit their patrimony. Like my father, however, they saw only their own purposes and would not hear me.

I swore I would go to Shechem and marry him merely in order that peace might be restored between our peoples. My brothers said they forbade it, but knowing it was the only way, I disobeyed them.

Shechem welcomed me and swore he loved me and would treat me tenderly. And so he did, when he was not in his cups. Whenever he was the worse for drink, however, he struck me repeatedly and cut me with his dagger. He would end by raping me, then falling asleep in a stupor. I would have taken my life but for the hope that my brothers would be brought to their senses if they thought I was well married.

In time, the torture became more than I could bear. One night, when Shechem lay on the cot drunk and satiated with lechery, I crept near and studied him. He was stretched on his back, his head halfway off the cot, his open mouth giving forth snores and belches. Blood flowed from my ear and from between my legs. I trembled as though cold. His hand held a clump of my hair, the dark hair the Canaanite women had said would make me the beloved of a great and good man one day. Carefully I removed the dagger from his scabbard. For a second, I caressed it, hesitating. Then I stabbed him in the throat.

Immense relief filled me, though I knew I had done wrong. I did not mind having to take my punishment. I sought Simeon and Levi in the fields and told them what I had done. They knew now that retribution on my behalf was unnecessary, for I had done the work myself, but they feared the retribution that would befall me and our people.

To protect me, and to protect our father and our tribe, they let it be broadcast that Shechem wished to be private in his tent because he had been circumcised. They also said that he had called for his people to follow him in performing the ritual. A proclamation was made, ordering every male to be circumcised. And when the men were sore from their wounds, Simeon and Levi mustered their men and slaughtered Shechem's followers. Because of what my brothers did, it was written in the chronicles of our people that they, and not I, were to blame for the violence which followed. Nobody ever knew that I had killed my husband and ravisher.

I am old now. I did not remarry, never bore children. When I go out among my people, the mothers point me out to their daughters and say that I fell in love with a Canaanite man and as a consequence was raped. That is a lesson, they say, to all girls who smile at men outside their own tribe. They say I was seductive, wore my hair uncovered and flirted with the young men. No wonder, they say, I got more than I bargained for.

I don't fault them for what they say. It soothes them to believe their virtue will protect them. Moreover, I am grateful, grateful to Simeon and Levi, who though they have lost their patrimony as a result of the slaughter, have taken me to live with their families in their tents. And I am grateful to God, who did not punish them, or me, with our lives.

AUTHOR'S NOTE

I wrote "The Rape of Dinah" during a meeting of the Women's Rosh Hodesh at my synagogue. As we studied Dinah's story, a *midrash* was cited that portrayed her as being in love with Shechem. Another midrash was needed, I felt, to acknowledge what we know about rape—that it is an act of violence. I also felt that the biblical account portrayed the thoughts and feelings of all characters except the central one, and I wished to redress that omission.

Dinah; daughter of Jacob and Leah

by Barbara D. Holender

Dina, the daughter whom Leah had borne to Jacob, went out to visit the daughters of the land. Shechem son of Hamor the Hivite . . . saw her, and took her and lay with her by force . . . in love with the maiden, he said to his father Hamor, "Get me this girl as a wife."

—Gen. 34:1-4

Why don't you kill me and be done with it?
My big brothers, my protectors—
Where were you when Shechem took me?
I cried out for you.

My father has four wives;
not one of them warned me of such things.
I have twelve brothers;
not one watched over me.
I have no sister
so I went to see the daughters of the land,
and Shechem found me. And forced me.

Where were you all those days
he kept me in his house?
I told him you would kill him,
but when you did not come, and he grew kind,
we fell in love, and then I said
I hoped you would be friends.

Still you did not come,
and Shechem's father went to Papa Jacob
with a marriage contract.

But when my love and all his men
took your covenant of circumcision
for my sake, to be one with you,

then you saved my honor
and slaughtered them
and spoiled their women

and brought me home
where no man will have me

and now you guard my tent.

AUTHOR'S NOTE

I wrote the midrash on Dinah at a time when rape was just
beginning to be discussed openly. The story disturbed me
greatly—it's a terrible tale. Dinah was twice victimized: by
the rapist, Shechem, and by her family. Family honor is all-
important in the story, and it is even now in Middle-Eastern
culture. Even Dinah's father, Jacob, was concerned not
about her but about the shame brought upon the family
and the threat of possible retaliation.

But the tale of Dinah resonates in a modern Western
context, and it was there that my *midrash* was found.

Leah's Eulogy

by Marla J. Feldman

They set out from Bethel; but when they were still some distance short of Ephrath, Rachel was in childbirth, and she had hard labor. When her labor was at its hardest, the midwife said to her, "Have no fear, for it is another boy for you." But as she breathed her last—for she was dying—she named him Ben-oni [son of my suffering]; but his father called him Benjamin [son of the right hand]. Thus Rachel died. She was buried on the road to Ephrath—now Bethlehem. Over her grave Jacob set up a pillar; it is the pillar at Rachel's grave to this day. Israel journeyed on, and pitched his tent beyond Migdal-eder."

—Gen. 35:16-21

I've torn my clothes, sat among the ashes, sprinkled the dust of the earth on your grave . . . Nothing helps, nothing lessens the loss I feel. How can I live with my grief?! For all our childish rivalry, there is no one in this world who knows me . . . knew me . . . like you, my little sister. O Rachel! Just when we should be enjoying the wealth of our years, you come to this bitter end. It's not fair.

I remember our childhood like it was yesterday. We were so different on the outside, yet so similar within. Though we were born only a few moments apart, I somehow became the "big" sister, and you, the baby of the family. I was larger, stronger, sturdy for bearing children, Father would say. When mother died I tended the hearth, looked after the family, kept our modest home; you thrived in the fresh air, playing among the sheep with the shepherd-boys. You were the pretty one, graceful and demure. You always knew how to get what you wanted from Father . . . he loved you best. He even allowed you to tend the herds you loved so—a young woman in the midst of a flock of men! I was jealous of your beauty and popularity . . . but I also admired your easy way with men and your adventurous spirit. You were always looking at the horizon, dreaming of other places.

When you saw Jacob at the well, you saw your chance to escape our pre-destined lives. He was an alluring traveler, a stranger and yet a suitable partner to please Father's ambitions for the family. So . . . you worked your womanly magic and he was smitten. His was a passion so consuming that he could see beauty in no other. He was your puppet and for seven years you teased him mercilessly. You could be so cruel. When Laban, our Father, proposed our prenuptial switch, I thought I would faint. I had secretly loved Jacob all those years, but could not betray my feelings for him lest I betray you. To this day, I do not know why Father insisted I marry first. Was it because he loved me or because propriety and custom demanded it? I sometimes wonder if he did it because he was ashamed of his homely, spinster daughter and was afraid that without deception I'd never find a husband.

When you agreed to help me deceive Jacob, I knew you did not love him as much as I did. You gave him up too easily. But I understood how trapped you must have felt, like one of your sheep caught in a thicket, yearning to be cared for but needing your freedom as much as air. You weren't prepared to give up your independence yet. I loved you for your generosity that day . . . but I also pitied you. For all your gifts, you would never be satisfied.

As much as I loved Jacob, I never felt good about the way we were married. He had to be blind-drunk to take me to his bed. I finally had my beloved, but his beloved was not his. In his heart, Jacob never really forgave us. It wasn't just because we deceived him. He awoke the morning of our marital bliss expecting his beloved Rachel by his side, and instead he found the cruel truth . . . you did not love him as he loved you. You could live without him.

Resigned and dejected, Jacob gave me the children for which I longed, but without the passion and love I yearned for. You were content to be left alone . . . until you saw the joy my sons gave me. For once it was your turn to be jealous. You couldn't stand that I had something you did not have. That I found happiness through my children. You turned on your charm and used all your wiles to gain a child, but Jacob had little sympathy. Our trick had quenched his passion, diminished his lust for you. In desperation you gave him your handmaid Bilhah and the ridiculous womb-contest began. My children, Bilhah's children, Zilpah's children . . . never yours. Exhausted, Jacob had to be coaxed, so I sent my children to find seductive potions . . . like the mandrakes you demanded from my first-born. Your jealousy backfired—I had more children and you remained barren, unfulfilled.

I confess that when I heard the screams of your first birth, I felt a quiet, evil pleasure. With Joseph's birth you would know some of the agony I had endured giving life to my seven. You would feel the heartache of raising a child, not knowing which path he would take. I'm sorry for those feelings. I regret the petty jealousy and anger that so diminished your youth. I had so much . . . why did I begrudge you this child? So much has happened since then—we've both changed. We have a new home in a new land, away from our father, away from the childhood rivalries that divided us. Jacob is finally home, at peace with himself and his past, perhaps ready to forgive and love again. We each have enough that we need not be jealous of one another. Wisdom finally caught up with us.

With this final birth, I found no pleasure in your screams. I prayed that out of your pain there would be born a child that would awaken our beloved's heart. I tried to comfort you in your last moments. I held you as you gave birth to your son with your dying breath. "It is another boy for you," I whispered. For you and not for me. I knew that Ben-Oni, the offspring of your pain, was destined to become Ben-Yamin, the child by his side, our husband's heart-song. This was the child Jacob would love and cherish over all the others. I knew that, and I was no longer jealous.

O Rachel, it's just not fair. How could you leave me, when we have so much left to share? I will miss you more than you could know. You are a part of me, the part that was not afraid, that was daring, bold, willful. And strong. The part that could show love. I will never be whole without you in my life. Without you, I no longer desire the man we married. I can no longer face the children who came between us. We have traveled our life-road together; I will not leave you now. I pledge to remain here the rest of my days. I will tend to your grave, even as Jacob moves on . . . too easily it seems. My tears will leave a pillar of salt to mark your final repose. Here you are buried, and here will I die. Together we will cry for our children.

ADDITIONAL REFERENCES

Although Leah and Rachel are described differently and referred to as "greater" (elder) and "smaller" (younger), there is a theme in midrashic literature that Leah and Rachel were twins. Their lives were destined to intertwine with the other twins, Esau and Jacob. The eldest, Esau and Leah, were to be married and the younger siblings, Jacob and Rachel, were to wed to each other. It is counted to Leah's credit that she had "weak eyes" from crying about her fate, not wishing to marry the wicked, slovenly Esau. It was to Rachel's credit that she permitted Jacob to be deceived in order to save her sister from such a fate. See Talmud Bavli, *Bava Batra* 123a; *Genesis Rabbah* 70:16; 71:2.

Now Laban had two daughters; the name of the older [bigger] one was Leah, and the name of the younger was Rachel. Leah had weak eyes; Rachel was shapely and beautiful.—Gen. 29:16-17.

So Jacob served seven years for Rachel and they seemed to him but a few days because of his love for her.—Gen. 29:20.

Laban said, "It is not the practice in our place to marry off the younger before the older."—Gen. 29:26.

To explain how Jacob could be fooled by Leah on his wedding night, the rabbis explained that Rachel had told Leah their secret signal and thus was an accomplice to the trickery. Some suggest that Rachel whispered to Jacob from outside the bridal chamber so he would not discover Leah's true identity. See Talmud Bavli, *Bava Batra* 123a; *Megilla* 13b.

When Rachel saw that she had borne Jacob no children, she became envious of her sister; and Rachel said to Jacob, "Give me children, or I shall die."—Gen. 30:1.

Leah had several children after Rachel traded a night with Jacob for Reuven's mandrakes.—Gen. 30:14ff.

A cry is heard in Ramah—wailing, bitter weeping—Rachel weeping for her children. She refuses to be comforted for her children, who are gone."—Jer. 31:15.

AUTHOR'S NOTE

In "Leah's Eulogy," Leah reflects upon the death of her younger sister Rachel. Much is made of Rachel's death in the biblical text, yet we hear nothing further about Leah. In a way, Rachel's death was Leah's as well. Their relationship mirrors that of many siblings, with love, jealousy, and admiration mingled with a host of other emotions.

Some classical *midrashim* presume Leah and Rachel to be twins, which explains Jacob's wedding night confusion. As an older twin myself, I identified with Leah and drew upon my personal experiences to envision the complexity of her relationship with Rachel.

A Genesis Kaddish

by Susan Gross

There they buried Abraham and Sarah his wife; there they
buried Isaac and Rebekah his wife; and there I buried Leah.
—Gen. 49:31

in memory of Adah
five generations after Cain
purifying generations
Adah, the mother of
tent-dwellers and cow-herders
who smell the dewed hay
and the mother of
pipe-players and lyre-strummers
who hear the meadow's song

in memory of Zillah
woman of shadows
and mother of
coppersmiths and iron-forgers
and of a daughter:

in memory of Naamah
six generations after Cain
aching to be pure again
but beaten
hair twisted eyes swollen
weilding angry earth-power

in memory of Reumah
who served and bore

Reumah means exalted
but by whom
by the yellow-headed flowers
which bow at your tent flap

in memory of Keturah
woman of incense
mother of multitudes
on the wrong side of the river
forever young
double of Hagar
sob-sister of Abishag
tending an old man's wrinkles

in memory of Judith
the first and forgotten
woman of barbs and thorns
sinking her spikes
into the Hittite hills

in memory of Basemath
woman of confusion
either Elon's daughter or Ishmael's
or neither
but bitter

in memory of Mahalath
true daughter of Ishmael
third wife of Esau
with a harp in your name
played by the wind
spilling over the mountaintops

in memory of Zilpah
annexed to the weak-eyed one
dropping child after child
into the soft brown earth
crowned with grass

in memory of Bilhah
stitched to the beauty
mother of stolen sons
mother of serpents
who bite horses' heels
and of sure-footed deer

in memory of Deborah
the first and forgotten
not the warrior but the nurse
who healed with honey
scooped from your own hive

in memory of Adah the second
fourth wife of Esau or first
second daughter of Elon or only
mother of god-gazers and -tramplers
a pretty ornament
hung on the willow tree

in memory of Oholibamah
oh holy high-place
woman of long legs and regal neck
daughter of Anah and Anah
your name is a clan a city a prayer

in memory of Anah
definite daughter
twin sister to your namesake
twin discoverer of the springs
which quenched the asses' thirst

in memory of Timna
one generation after Esau
sister of hiders
mother of fighters
who lost and drowned in blood

in memory of Mehetabel
queen of tinkling bells
their clappers flung during dances
in honor of dark divinities
lurking in palace walls
daughter of your mother:

in memory of Matred
inching forward
squeezing a foot a toe
even a toenail
through the door of history
a heavy genealogical door
threatening to clamp shut

in memory of Asenath
woman of secrets
never exposed or aborted
but ferried to Egypt
and adopted
blooming as a priest's daughter
mother of the sudden-blessed

in memory of Serah
bringer of the sweet news
woman of the forced march
sister of the seventy men
last of the named

ADDITIONAL REFERENCES

Lamech took to himself two wives: the name of the one was
Adah . . . —Gen. 4:19
    Now the man knew his wife Eve, and she conceived and
bore Cain . . . —Gen. 4:1

Adah bore Jabal; he was the ancestor of those who dwell in tents and amidst herds.—Gen. 4:20

And the name of his brother was Jubal; he was the ancestor of all who play the lyre and the pipe.—Gen. 4:21

. . . and the name of the other was Zillah.—Gen. 4:19

As for Zillah, she bore Tubal-cain, who forged all implements of copper and iron.—Gen. 4:22

And the sister of Tubal-cain was Naamah.—Gen. 4:22

And his concubine, whose name was Reumah, also bore children: Tebah, Gaham, Tahash, and Maacah.—Gen. 22:24

Abraham took another wife, whose name was Keturah.—Gen. 25:1

So Sarai, Abram's wife, took her maid, Hagar the Egyptian . . . and gave her to her husband Abram as concubine.—Gen. 16:3

They found Abishag the Shunammite and brought her to the king. The girl was exceedingly beautiful. She became the king's attendant . . . —I Kings 1:3-4

When Esau was forty years old, he took to wife Judith daughter of Beeri the Hittite . . . —Gen. 26:34

. . . and Basemath daughter of Elon the Hittite . . . —Gen. 26:34

Esau took wives from among the Canaanite women . . . and also Basemath daughter of Ishmael and sister of Nebaioth.—Gen. 36:1-3

So Esau went to Ishmael and took to wife, in addition to the wives he had, Mahalath the daughter of Ishmael, sister of Nebaioth.—Gen. 28:9

Laban had given his maidservant Zilpah to his daughter Leah as her maid.—Gen. 29:24

Laban had given his maidservant Bilhah to his daughter Rachel as her maid.—Gen. 29:29

Dan shall be a serpent by the road, a viper by the path, that bites the horse's heels so that his rider is thrown backward.—Gen. 49:17

Naphtali is a hind let loose, which yields lovely fawns.—Gen. 49:21

Deborah, Rebekah's nurse, died, and was buried under the oak below Bethel . . . —Gen. 35:8

Deborah, wife of Lappidoth, was a prophetess; she led Israel at that time.—Judges 4:4

Esau took his wives from among the Canaanite women— Adah daughter of Elon the Hittite . . . —Gen. 36:2

. . . and Oholibamah daughter of Anah daughter of Zibeon the Hivite . . . —Gen. 36:2

. . . Anah *daughter* of Zibeon the Hivite . . . Gen. 36:2

. . . the Anah who discovered the hot springs in the wilderness while pasturing the asses of *his* father Zibeon.—Gen. 36:24 [emphasis mine]

Timna was a concubine of Esau's son Eliphaz; she bore Amalek to Eliphaz.—Gen. 36:13

. . . and his wife's name was Mehetabel . . . —Gen. 36:39

. . . daughter of Matred daughter of Me-zahab.—Gen. 36:39

. . . and he gave him for a wife Asenath daughter of Potiphera, priest of On.—Gen. 41:45

Asher's sons: Imnah, Ishvah, Ishvi, and Beriah, and their sister Serah.—Gen. 46:17

AUTHOR'S NOTE

Midrash is a method of interpreting the biblical narrative so that it becomes meaningful to modern readers. The biblical text itself is often very sparse, devoid of lush description and emotion. By inserting descriptive and emotive elements into the text, the midrashist can force the ancient words to address contemporary agenda. My work can be pegged as feminist *midrash*, because I attempt to create out of the Hebrew Bible empowering messages for women. Because the biblical text has an overwhelmingly patriarchal tone, the usable portions for feminists are at times well hidden. Sometimes feminist *midrash* requires simply naming the unnamed.

Jochebed, Mother of Moses

by Barbara D. Holender

The daughter of Pharaoh . . . spied the basket among the reeds . . . When she opened it she saw that it was a child . . . and said, "This must be a Hebrew child." Then his sister said . . . "Shall I go and call you a Hebrew nurse to suckle the child for you?" . . . So the girl went and called the child's mother.

—Ex. 2:1-10

Baby, you have mothers three,
   lulla lullaby,
one to watch you, one to nurse you,
one to take you away from me.

> *This new Egyptian mother of yours*
> *pays me to care*
> *for my forbidden son.*
> *Is it possible*
> *she does not know who I am?*

One little cry, one little cry,
   lulla lullaby,
now you're prince of Egypt, love,
and I'm no better than a slave.

> *Your sister's eyes cannot meet mine*
> *because you were discovered;*
> *yet how cleverly she keeps us*
> *together this little while.*

And what if we should meet one day?
   lulla lullaby
Will you be my enemy?
Pharaoh's daughter's little boy?

> *How can I tell you who you are?*
> *God knows what she told her father.*
> *What if he turns on you—*
> *who will save you?*

Where you go I will be.
   lulla lullaby
Though you bear a stranger's name
mama's blood and papa's seed
will bring you home.

AUTHOR'S NOTE

Miriam needed Jochebed as antecedent. And Jochebed herself had much to say about putting her baby at risk, giving him up either to death or the enemy. What heartache and anxiety she must have felt. Loss and reunion were the pattern her life with Moses was to take. I found the echo in alternating her own reflections with the lullaby to her baby. And her thoughts about her daughter set the stage for Miriam's opening words.

The First Step

by Nancy Ellen Roth

The woman conceived and bore a son; and when she saw how beautiful he was, she hid him for three months. When she could hide him no longer, she got a wicker basket for him and caulked it with bitumen and pitch. She put the child into it and placed it among the reeds by the bank of the Nile. And his sister stationed herself at a distance, to learn what would befall him."

—Ex. 2:2-4

I am crouching in the mud, high on the river bank. The tall grasses hide me. The sun is high and hot. My legs are stiff from stooping, but I am not thinking of that. I am thinking about my family.

My mother brought us here at daybreak, my two brothers and me. One of my brothers went back with her. The other one, the baby, she put in the water. Not for a bath, no, she put him in a little cradle boat that she had made out of rushes and mud.

I have never seen her as she was this morning. First she gave the baby some milk, and when she was finished she put him on her shoulder to help the milk settle in his stomach. These things she does all the time. But then she began to cry. She covered her face and made no sound but I knew she was crying. It scared me. I almost ran away. My little brother Aaron did run away. But I stayed. I wanted to see what would happen next.

My mother kissed the baby and laid him in the little boat. He kicked his foot and made a baby sound.

"See, he likes it," I said. I was trying to help my mother stop crying.

She did not stop crying but she did smile a little. She touched the baby's cheek and he smiled too. Then she fitted a bulrush cover over the cradle boat to shade the baby and put the boat in the water. She pushed it gently away from the bank but it did not go far, bobbing among the short flag reeds near the river's edge. I could not see the baby but I could hear him making sleepy little noises as he rocked in his boat. It looked like fun.

"May I get in the boat too?" I asked. My mother was silent. She did not even look at me.

"Aaron! See the baby in the little boat!" I called.

My brother came running. He did not stop at the water. He splashed right in and fell face forward in a muddy place. "Want a boat!" he blubbered as my mother yanked him out of the river. "Boat for me!"

My mother sighed and hauled him away from the water. Aaron shouted and tried to wriggle free. "Want a boat for me! For me!" She carried him farther from the river. I thought she would put him down, but she kept walking toward home.

I ran after her a little way. "Where are you going? The baby is here, Mother!"

"Come, Miriam," she said, barely turning her head. She walked faster.

Come? Was I supposed to bring the baby? I looked for the boat. It had floated down the river a bit, and now appeared to be stuck among some taller reeds. I ran down and plunged in the water. The river was deeper and muddier than I had thought. A few steps in, my feet suddenly sank in mud up to my ankles. The water flowed around my waist. I could go no farther. I called my mother but she did not come.

Where was my mother? I cried again for help but there was no answer.

I saw then that the baby's boat, still lodged among the reeds, was out of my reach. My mother was gone. I wiped off my tears and tried to lift my foot. To my surprise it came up easily, and so I was able to struggle back to the land.

I dragged myself up the bank, meaning to go home. At the top of the bank I turned one last time to look at the baby's boat. There it was, hiding in the river. I did not want to leave it. So I sat down in the tall grasses. I would hide too. I wanted to see what would happen.

That was a long time ago now. The sun is in the highest part of the sky, beating down on my head and hurting my eyes. I am wondering why my mother has not come back.

She is acting strangely of late, not talking, not letting me or Aaron near her. Yesterday when she was weaving the bulrushes to make the baby's boat she did not even stop to feed us. I had to get my own food and some for Aaron too. Only the baby seemed to interest her. She held him and sang to him while we watched from the corner. He got milk and love; we got none. I find I am a little angry about that.

I am very angry. Yesterday I was angry too, I remember. Aaron was crying in my lap and I was wishing the baby would disappear.

Then I am confused. Mother loves the baby, why did she leave him in the river? And why did she not come back when I called her? Why is she not coming now?

Something is wrong. Something is wrong in my family. It hurts to think about this so I try to stop. I look again toward the baby's boat but the sun's glare on the water hurts my eyes. Hurt, hurt, hurt. Everything hurts.

Here is a new sound. Women are singing. I hear their voices but I do not see them. There they are. They are Egyptian women walking along the river and singing. The song is happy. I do not know their language perfectly but I think it is about . . . bathing? Yes, that is why they have come to the river. But there are so many of them, perhaps eight or ten. Since when can so many women walk freely together, singing?

One among them is wearing much golden jewelry. Her face is painted. She is not singing, just walking. The others surround her, carrying many small bundles. They sing, it seems, to her.

Now they stop on a flat sandy bank that extends into the river. One sets out a chair and the golden woman sits on it. Two of the women, her maids, kneel and begin to remove the bracelets from her wrists. The others begin a new song. Some of them dance a little, and clap. I like their dance and wonder if I could do it. And I like the song.

Another sound rings out from the river. I am amazed, it is so loud that even I, up here, can hear it. It is the baby in his little boat, crying.

The women also hear it. They break off singing and look toward the river. The baby gathers his breath, then howls, howls, like a hungry wild cat.

I am frightened. We should not be here, my brother and I. Mother says the Egyptian king, the Pharaoh, does not like us, we who are not Egyptian. "Some of his people could hurt you, so be careful of them," my mother told me. Once she told me who we are but I forget now. We are not Egyptian.

The golden woman points to the little boat and one of her maidens wades into the water. She has no trouble walking in the river. Perhaps I should try again to rescue the baby.

I run down the bank. My feet are prickly from crouching so long. I stumble among the reeds by the river, which suddenly seem thicker and taller around me. I cannot make my way through them until after the Egyptian woman retrieves the boat and brings it to the golden woman. The reeds open before me then. I see the golden woman remove the cover and lift out my weeping baby brother. She holds him close, murmuring in her language. I creep nearer and hear her say, "This is one of the Hebrews' children."

Hebrews, yes. They name us after our language, my mother told me that. They do not exactly know who we are, my mother said. Israel's children. That is who we are. I remember now.

My brother will not stop wailing. The women take turns trying to comfort him. They look kindly, but they do not know my brother. He needs milk from his mother.

I am afraid to step out of my hiding place. They are not helpless, they are grown up. One of them must be able to think what to do.

My brother is frantic. His cries pull me. I cannot stand still anymore. I sweep aside the reeds and take one step toward the Egyptian women. Then I must go the rest of the way.

The golden woman is sitting in her chair, the baby in her arms. He is beating on her chest, searching for milk. As I approach I notice how her smooth black hair shines in the bright sunlight. I touch my tangled muddy hair and feel a little ashamed. She raises her eyebrows and I stop where I stand.

"Perhaps the baby is hungry?" I say in my best Egyptian. I pretend to nurse the baby as my mother does.

The golden woman frowns and says something to her women and one of them says in Hebrew, "The daughter of Pharaoh says that the baby is hungry."

"Shall I call a Hebrew woman to nurse the child for you?" I ask in Hebrew.

The golden woman hears the translation and says, "Go."

I race like the running river to my home. I am breathless when I arrive. My mother gives me a sour look as I spill out the story. She shakes her head but she comes with me. I try to hurry but she will not be rushed. She does not really believe me. But near the river, when she hears the baby's cries, she starts to run. Then she sees the Egyptian women and halts. There is her baby in the golden woman's lap. I hear my mother gasp. She lowers her eyes.

The daughter of Pharaoh beckons her forward. "Take this child away and nurse him for me," she says, "and I will pay you wages." One of her maidens takes the baby from her and hands him to my mother.

The Egyptian maiden repeats the words in Hebrew and adds, "The daughter of Pharaoh has found the boy-child in the water and wishes to adopt him. She will call him "Moses." When he is older she will bring him to her palace. He will be under the protection of Pharaoh while you are caring for him."

Mother gives the baby some milk and he quiets. The princess watches from her chair. She seems pleased. She instructs the maiden to escort us home and pay my mother.

As we walk up from the river I feel a light touch on my back. I am surprised, for my mother has not touched me for many days. She smiles at me and passes. Over her shoulder my brother fixes his alert eyes on my face. In silent relief I watch him from behind my mother. All the way home his eyes are turned toward mine.

ADDITIONAL REFERENCE

Then Miriam the prophetess, Aaron's sister, took a timbrel in her hand, and all the women went out with her in dance with timbrels.—Ex. 15:20

AUTHOR'S NOTE

As a student of the *Tanakh* I read and write midrash to illuminate and tease apart strands of meaning from the thick twine of literary traditions from which the narratives are derived. Perhaps, in the process, I weave in a strand or two of my own—as did the midrashic scholars of old.

Miriam's story has gripped me since childhood. After becoming a parent, I found new reasons to be intrigued by her compassionate and decisive action on behalf of her family. In stepping out from the safe cover of the reeds, Miriam begins an uncertain journey that will culminate in the Exodus. Traditional midrash seemed to miss the significance of Miriam's act of *chesed,* or generosity, toward a weaker party, Moses, and its implications for the Israelites' passage out of a state of bondage.

Moses Goes Exploring

by Adam Fisher

. . . when Moses had grown up, he went out to his kinsfolk and witnessed their labors. He saw an Egyptian beating a Hebrew, one of his kinsmen.

—Ex. 2:11

When Moses was growing up in Pharaoh's palace, he had a wonderful time. The palace itself was made up of long halls and secret hiding places. There were dogs and cats to play with. There were even monkeys whom he taught to do tricks. And, he had his very own horse.

Any time he wanted to go someplace, like down to the Great River, he could get on his horse and go. He often played with Egyptian kids. They knew that he came from the Israelites but they didn't seem to care. The princess who raised him was very nice and Pharaoh never bothered him.

As he got older, he went more and more places on his own. One day he took some food and got on his horse and went off exploring. All his life, he could see the pyramids being built off in the distance but he had never seen them up close.

After a few hours of riding, he got to the pyramids. He was amazed at how big they were. He was fascinated by the precise way they were being constructed. He also noticed that there were hundreds, thousands of people carrying heavy rocks, moving soil, cutting tremendous stones. Then he looked closer at the people. They looked very thin; some of them begged for food. Some looked sick. Sometimes they just passed out in the hot sun, because there was no water there. The guards would whip them until they either got up or died.

Moses started to shake. He'd always been told that the slaves were well treated and lived a good life. They had treated him well but they had lied to him about how they treated his people. He was enraged and confused. He wanted to help but he didn't know what to do.

Moses turned his horse around and rode sadly back to the palace. At first he tried to forget what he had seen. He tried to pretend it was a bad dream. He told himself that there was nothing he could do. But he was troubled. He didn't sleep at night because he kept thinking of ways that he might help.

Moses' best friend was an Israelite servant in the palace. He was an older boy, named Elya. When Moses told him what he had seen, Elya sadly replied that there was nothing Moses could do. There were too many who were hungry, too many who were thirsty. Pharaoh would not allow the slaves to be given any help and Moses would only get into trouble for even mentioning it.

But Moses could not stop thinking about it. He had some friends among the Egyptian kids. One, named Ra, was a good friend. When Moses told him what he had seen, Ra told him, "Mind your own business. You can't do anything. Just be glad you have it good and enjoy life." Moses was furious. "How could he tell me to enjoy life when my people were treated so badly."

Moses could not eat and could not sleep. He lost weight. His face looked gray. An old Israelite woman who was also a servant in the palace took him aside and asked what was troubling him. He found a place where no one would hear them, and he told her everything he had seen. She said, "Moses, you are free. And you can help our people. Pharaoh isn't going to free the slaves and stop building the pyramids. But you must try to help. You must try to do what you can. This is my plan."

The next day, he went out to the pyramids and spoke to the man in charge. The man complained to him that the building was behind schedule because he couldn't get the slaves to work faster. Moses said, "Maybe if you gave them enough food and water they'd be better workers." The man kept saying that the people were slaves and he shouldn't treat them any better. Moses kept telling him that the slaves would work better if they had enough to eat and drink. It wasn't easy, but the man in charge figured that

Moses was a prince in Pharoah's house, so he listened. That is how Moses helped his people long before he could free them.

AUTHOR'S NOTE

Even though he could not free his people at first, Moses was able to help them. He learned then what the rabbis taught many years later: we are not required to heal every hurt and every injustice, but we are required to try. For those who save one life, it is as if they have saved the whole world.

This is why the Torah first tells us that, ". . . when Moses had grown up, he went out to his kinsfolk and witnessed their labors. He saw an Egyptian beating a Hebrew, one of his kinsmen." Only later, in the next verse (Ex. 2:12), do we read that ". . . he struck down the Egyptian . . ." and saved the Hebrew. After that, God said to Moses, "I will send you to Pharaoh that you may bring forth My people, the people of Israel out of Egypt." (Ex. 3:10)

Sing a Lively Song

by Peter Lovenheim

*Then Moses and the Israelites sang this song to the Lord.
They said: I will sing to the Lord for He has triumphed
gloriously; /Horse and driver He has hurled into the sea.*
                                                    —Ex. 15:1

*Then Miriam the prophetess, Aaron's sister, took a timbrel in
her hand, and all the women went out after her in dance with
timbrels. And Miriam chanted for them, "Sing to the Lord, for
He has triumphed gloriously; /Horse and driver He has
hurled into the sea."*
                                                   —Ex. 15:20

After their close escape from Egypt, the Israelites gathered in
small groups on the shore of Sinai to rest. In the middle of one
group, a young man who had brought a guitar strummed a few
minor chords. Responding to the music, the people began to sing.
They sang slow, meaningful songs they had learned in Egypt—
songs that had helped sustain them through the long, painful
years of slavery.

The first song was a favorite, an early Israelite version of
"Scarborough Fair."

> Are you going to scare the old Pharaoh?
> Blood, frogs, lice—-hail, lightening are fine.
> Remember me to one who rules there,
> He once was a captor of mine.

This was followed by an old Israelite protest song:

> How many stones must a man carry up
> Before he can see the sky?
> And how many stones must a man carry up
> Before he can hear people cry?

They were into the seventh verse of:

> Where have all the Pharaohs gone?
> Long time passing—

when Moses approached. He listened for only half a minute.

"Stop! Stop!" he cried, walking to the middle of the song circle. "Why are you singing dirges? This is no time for dirges!"

The people looked with dull, tired eyes at their leader. No one seemed to know what Moses was talking about.

"What are dirges?" a young man asked.

"Dirges are songs about grief, sad things," explained Moses. "This is a happy time. Why would you want to sit around singing dirges?"

"We like these songs," protested a woman. "They mean a lot to us."

"Of course they do," said Moses, "but let's hear you sing something with a little life in it!"

Moses had not anticipated how much the group would resent his suggestion.

Among the singers, a young bearded man with sensitive brown eyes seemed to speak for the rest: "You don't understand, Moses. There's pain in the world. There's poverty, and children without food. There are wars, and people in prison. We were slaves so we know what it feels like to be oppressed and to suffer. Just because we're free now, doesn't mean we can turn our backs on everyone else in the world who is suffering and just go have a good time."

A murmur of assent ran through the crowd.

"These songs are about injustice," the young man continued, "injustice that is real—even if you don't like to hear about it."

It was at this moment that Moses realized that physically liberating his people from Egypt might have been easy compared to liberating their spirit.

"What you say is true," Moses responded, "but celebrating our own good fortune doesn't mean we don't care about others or that we want to deny or forget their suffering. Right now we are free, and safe on dry land, and we can celebrate this moment and our lives and the glory of God who brought us to this great day."

"Friends," continued Moses, "can we sing a lively song to celebrate?"

But the people could not think of any lively songs.

So Moses taught the Israelites a new song of triumph and life. It had a quick rhythm, lively phrasing, and a beat you could dance to.

"I will sing to the Lord, for He has triumphed gloriously," they sang. And as they sang, their spirits lifted. And then Miriam came with her tambourine to lead everyone in dance. She sang: "Sing to the Lord, for He has triumphed gloriously."

AUTHOR'S NOTE

In the late 1960s, while visiting the United States from his native England, Rabbi Percival Goldberg took to task our post-confirmation class for its tendency to sing meaningful but mournful protest songs of the era—what he called "dirges." He said we were young, healthy, and free, and should express our good fortune by singing livelier songs. He said doing so would make us feel better. He was right.

To Rabbi Goldberg, this *midrash* is dedicated. May his memory be for a blessing.

Moses and the Ten Contractual Provisions

by Alan K. Posner

The Lord came down upon Mt. Sinai, on the top of the mountain, and the Lord called Moses . . . and Moses went up . . . And God spoke [in thunder] all these words, saying: I the Lord am your God who brought you out of the land of Egypt, the house of bondage: You shall have no other gods beside Me.

—Ex. 19:20; 20:1-3

And Moses heard the thunder and, in a quivering voice, said to the LORD: "If I might interrupt . . . I believe that you know my attorney, Max Finkelstein." A small man in a double-breasted suit stepped forward to face the thunder and began to speak: "Now I don't expect that we will have any other gods beside you, LORD. And I'm sure that many of the other provisions of this contract are fine, but Moses and I would like some time to review the entire tablet before we agree to any one section. Let me put it this way, I think we can easily end up with a win/win situation here, but it may take a little time and discussion. By the way, are you represented by counsel?"

The LORD, resisting the old joke about all lawyers ending up with the Devil, turned to Moses and with even greater lightning and thunder said: "You have seen what I did to the Egyptians, how I bore you on eagles' wings and brought you to me. Now then, if you will obey me faithfully and keep my covenant, you shall be my treasured possession among all peoples. And by the way, I really don't think you need your own attorney, Moses, to obtain that favorable result."

Moses summoned his courage and responded: "Well, to be honest, I go way back with Max. You may remember that situation in Egypt with frogs, lice, insects and the like. Max jumped right in and defended me. I'm not sure that we would ever have been allowed to leave the Egyptian jurisdiction if it had not been for Max."

The LORD continued: "I have been through the no other God than me introduction, right? Another thing I am really against would be making a sculptured image, or any likeness of what is in the heavens above or on the earth below or in the waters under the earth. You shall not bow down to them or serve them, for I the LORD your God am an impassioned God, visiting the guilt of the parents upon the children, upon the third and the fourth generations of those who reject me, but showing kindness to the thousandth generation of those who love me and keep my commandments."

"If I can interrupt you on this one, LORD," Max inquired. "I think this whole guilt thing is inflammatory. Once Moses makes a deal, he will live with it. We don't need any penalty provision that *assumes* we are going to violate the contract. And let me just say right now that my client does not have any intention of making any kind of sculptured image, right Mo?" Moses nodded his head. "In any event, LORD, Moses and I are interested in hearing the remaining provisions of the Agreement."

The LORD continued: "Honor your Father and your Mother, that you may long endure on the land that the LORD your God is assigning to you. You shall not murder. You shall not commit adultery. You shall not steal. You shall not bear false witness against your neighbor. You shall not covet your neighbor's house. You shall not covet your neighbor's wife, or his male or female slave, or his ox or his ass, or anything that is your neighbor's."

"If I could interrupt you one more time, LORD," Max said. Moses and Max whispered for a moment and then Max spoke: "These provisions seem reasonable and appropriate, but we do have a few questions. Coveting your neighbor's wife and house . . . what exactly do you mean by "neighbor?" For that matter, what do you really mean by "covet?" Mo doesn't have a house or neighbor right now, but in the future he may well end up in a large subdivision with different levels of housing. I mean suppose that Jethro decides to buy Mo and Zipporah the basic three-bedroom ranch, while across the street Aaron and his family are in a four-bedroom model with a deck and a panelled family room. Are we saying here that if Moses wants to save up to get himself a four-bedroom job, he is going to be in trouble with you?" What are we talking about here? Also, why is adultery right up there with murder? Shouldn't they really be in different provisions? And what about mutual releases for any commandment violations to date? Not that any have necessarily occurred. And what about . . ."

Suddenly the mountain top was consumed in fire. And Moses and Max looked to the fire and Max said with urgency: "OK. Listen, these are not deal breakers. I'm just trying to understand the fine points. Actually, it looks like this might not be a good time for you, LORD. Why don't I speak further with Mo and we will get back to you." With that, they quickly descended the mountain.

And it came to pass that, after those forty days and forty nights, the Lord gave Moses two tablets of stone which did not contain liquidated damages sections, escape clauses or other contractual provisions. Instead, they set forth the Lord's Commandments.

And suddenly, Moses had two important insights. First, he understood that we are to reflect on the Lord's teachings; we are to feel them with all of our heart and soul; and we must follow them to our fullest ability. But those teachings are *Commandments.* In no circumstance are they negotiable. Nor can they be revised, amended or deleted. Second, Moses realized that a lawyer is not necessarily helpful in every situation. But, if you really need one, perhaps you should try a big firm near Horeb.

AUTHOR'S NOTE

As a practicing attorney for nearly twenty-five years, I was drawn to Moses, the lawgiver. His "legal" contribution has had an enormous influence on the development of Judaism. That contribution, when viewed in the context of our modern litigious society, led me inexorably to two questions: Who was the

law giver's lawyer? What would have happened if today's attor-
neys had represented Moses at that most crucial of times. The
result is a midrash about the arrival before the Lord of Moses
with his own personal attorney who is determined to obtain the
best deal for his client.

Letters on Both Sides

by Martin W. Levy

Moses turned and went down from the mountain bearing the two tablets of the Pact, tablets inscribed on both their surfaces: they were inscribed on the one side and on the other. The tablets were God's work, and the writing was God's writing, incised upon the tablets.

—Ex. 32:15–16

Moses scaled the parched terrain carrying a goatskin sack and a water gourd. The jagged rocks cut his swollen feet. Robed in heavy sheepskins, his sash fastened with copper and bone, he squinted at the dawn's amber eyelids. His wife Zipporah had stitched a thick sandal from leather and calfskin, which provided protection from the rough granite. But the sharp crevices hobbled his labored steps. The leather thongs cut into his callused ankles. A morning star blinked with spongy whiteness. What message would come as he reached the summit? How would he carry this message back to the people? In the early light he spotted cactus stalks poking over limestone outcroppings. Moses cut the plump stalk and squeezed the warm sap over his wounds.

He sang to God as the day's journey took him across a bald mountain, surrounded by desert and parched wadis. He hummed, *nesher kinafayich,* "on the wings of eagles," for he knew the Holy One would lift him up. A week earlier, he couldn't imagine the searing winds as he sat with the elders at the camp. With parched lips he sang of an eagle's majestic wings, wailing families and the promise of a land flowing with milk and honey.

Moses dreamed of the camp where herdsmen offered goat's milk and ointment for his legs. He walked slowly, soothed by cool waters and pungent grasses. The gray haze of the fiery clouds surrounded the camp as he slept under a shepherd's watchful gaze. The pillar of fire blazed above while at his feet, field mice and spiders crawled. A sheepskinned human was rare in these mountains.

Dreams enveloped him. Aaron directed the camp's elders and listened as the princes recited triumphant stories of chariots being sucked into a watery abyss. Aaron admonished them, recounting that only God's might had led them to freedom. Sister Miriam danced with the women as they beat their tambourines and clicked copper timbrels. Her followers twirled slender marsh sticks and wailed as she coaxed sounds from the ram's horn. She sang God's praises, beseeching the Holy One to reveal new springs of water.

Moses wrapped his tunic across his neck and dreamed of murmurers crying against Aaron: "Where is our leader, where is this invisible redeemer?" The princes grumbled: "Is Moses the only one who speaks with God? God redeemed us all, were those not your words?" they cried to Aaron.

Awake, Moses sipped from his goatskin pouch. The Pleaides dazzled the sky, while clumps of frost weighted the cactus. He prayed that the new day would bring food and the mysterious words of the One who led him past Pharoah's armies. Coaxing precious water from his gourd, he tied a damp cloth around his neck. Words of anguish and doubt streamed from his unmoving lips. The rocks cut him, yet he wound the leather sandals even tighter.

By afternoon, Moses reached the summit and rested. He slaked his thirst on cactus juice. With the morning's sweet frost, Moses pretended it was honey. Under the jagged limestone overhang he fashioned a pillow of twigs, goatskin, and cactus ears. Moses scoured the summit for a remnant of morning frost. He lay down and dreams carried him to the Israelite camp. He tasted cream from goat's milk and washed away the gnats knotted in his beard. From the women's camp he heard, "Moses is lost, let us go back to Egypt. Our Moses is lost," they chanted.

That night a storm swallowed all, the wind searing his body. Moses curled himself into a hollow, tucking the goatskin around his legs. After three months of rocks and dust, the people below felt the anger of a desert storm. Hail the size of quail eggs pelted them. He pressed against the limestone cover with his staff, digging with his nails into the soft stone, slowly carving out a small cavern for protection. His coat was soaked with ice and sleet. Near his feet he shaped the limestone into a tiny basin, collecting water for the next day. As the storm passed, he dreamed that the Israelites were pelting him with stones. He awoke to find sharp welts across his legs. A column of ants marched across his ankle, filing towards the limestone basin. There they encircled a drowned squirrel. Moses grabbed the prey and bathed it in the yellowish water. He gathered wet twigs and uncovered the dry seeds and branches he'd carefully wrapped in the bottom of his pouch. With his flint he kindled a sparse fire, preparing his first dinner in more than a week. He eased his thirst with mouthfuls of hail crusted on a granite slab.

The sun warmed the cool granite and Moses turned east, shielding his eyes and bowing towards the aquamarine-framed mountains. As he prayed, asking God for strength, a sheet of limestone cracked, sheering off a three-foot slab. With his wind-burned arms, he balanced the rock upon his knees. The mica glints dazzled him. "God of our fathers, and God of our mothers, our Redeemer and Savior, what shall I tell my people?" In a hoarse voice, he cried: "You who whip the winds, for You the thunder claps, You fill the oases, now fill me with a message. Master of the heavens and Creator of the dawn, unveil Your voice. I did not journey to the mountain to meet death."

Then Moses lifted the limestone and set it on a sheet of granite. A voice echoed in his head as he grasped a pebble and swept it across the limestone, pressing and chiselling. His muscles tensed and sweat poured from his neck as he carved a message—words he'd never heard before. In a few minutes, the rock was complete with short phrases. His hands shook, sweat soaked his goatskin and his eyes watered from the noon glare. He prayed, "Thank You for giving me this day and bringing us to freedom."

The limestone sparkled with mica-flecked letters. Exhausted by the fevered writing, he set aside his chisel and watched the sun's climb over the limestone peaks. As he gazed at this mysterious message, he remembered sounds from the burning bush: "I will be who I will be." The letters swam across his sight in a crescendo of fiery lights. He touched each letter, and traced the stone as an invisible pressure pressed against his fingers from the other side. He lifted the limestone and the very letters were etched on both sides. With the newly fashioned words he copied the phrases in the damp dirt. He read, "I am the Lord your God, who brought you out of the land of Egypt . . ." And as he read, a pulse of invisible heat flowed through Moses' gnarled hands.

Under a limestone overhang, he rested from the noon sun, tracing these words over and over. Grateful, Moses began his descent.

AUTHOR'S NOTE

The words of Exodus are laden with metaphors, which allowed me to rethink the idea that God gave the tablets to Moses inscribed on both sides of the stone. Elsewhere in the Torah, we find a repetition of the idea that God engraved the Ten Words with the divine finger. This idea captures the artistic imagination, demanding that we interpret what Moses actually wrote and what part God plays in enabling Moses to write. For me, Moses' hands become an extension of divine power, as if the divine will pulses through the human vehicle. The text proposes a host of questions that can be addressed best through the modern midrashic process.

The Material Calf

by Diane Simkin Demeter

As he approached the camp, Moses saw the calf and the dancing, and he was angry; he flung the tablets down, and they were shattered to pieces at the foot of the mountain. Then he took the calf they had made and burnt it; he ground it to powder, sprinkled it on water, and made the Israelites drink it.

—Ex. 32:19–21

Aaron never prepared me. I'm used to accolades, adoration, worship . . . what's this? My God! (or is to use His name too great an irony) to be dragged through the desert, spit at, scorned, beaten like a common paltroon, a paltry beggar, a two-bit thief??

Such a fuss about a *bissel gelt,* as Aaron would say. A little idol. Little *moi?* Tell me, what's so bad? My sleaky golden flanks, my udder glistening with riches beyond your wildest dreams . . . ever.

This noisy rabble is babbling about the one true Lord, the miraculous, the "immanent," but I'd like to ask you something; what about—the REAL!!! Melt me down, and you *got* something! Oooo yeah! Just milk me, baby, you never heard a "moo" like mine. And I can be *touched*—indeed, I encourage a little pat, tickle or pop now and then—and who hasn't heard about the *taste* and *smell* of solid gold? Yes, I'm a perfectly credible edible. A great candidate. So why this? This marching procession in the baking desert in which I am mocked, vilified, bombarded by rocks, where once I was carried aloft . . . and, dare I say it? . . . loved.

Trust me. I *am* the senses. But—this is rather a painful *but* and, if the truth be told, I usually don't dwell in painful buts—there *is* one area in which I happen to be deficient. I can't talk. But hey, who's perfect? And what's so great about the *WORD?* I mean I know how you all **love** the *word,* but, bottom line, where does it get you? I got *udders* to offer: I drive men wild—ladies, too, if given half the chance. So wake up and smell the coffee, boys! I'm the Earth Mother, a real hot mama—a little dust, a little lust, a little glamor, and some weekend heat. . . . Ooooo yeah . . .

So whatcha gonna do? You want Law, with a capital "L," you want Order, with a capital "O"? You want responsibility, civility, conversation? BORING!!!! I mean, is there no place for a little getaway behind a rock? Come on, come on, come on, you wanna be dour, sour, tough and ride the road of obedience, loyalty? Hey! A girl just wants to have fun!

Have I asked the wrong question?

Yea, though I travel down this dark and dusty path, suffering the slings and arrows of outrageous fortune, I say, wait a minute, there. WAIT A MINUTE!!!! It's a *choice,* isn't it? But . . . **does it have to be?** I mean, couldn't we have a little regulation during the week and a little *de*regulation at its end? I'm an expert on ends, and I, for one, think it would be great! Why does this have to be *my* end, anyhow, now that we're talking about ends?

Now I know it's not fashionable to whine and "why me" in front of everybody, but these are rather dire circumstances. Pardon the cowboy expression, but, *I'm soon to bite the dust!* And though you may not have heard of cowboys, they're just like you ('cept they're wandering in a different desert), and *they* like to have fun! So listen up! Listen up there! Why me??? Is it that Aaron fashioned me? Not the brother with the weight and stature, of "burning bush" fame, you know—Moses? Think about it. Search your souls. I'm young, I'm cute, I'd be a great Godhead! I just can't talk, that's all. That damn *word,* you know . . . the power of the *word?* OH HELP! HELP! HELP!!! OH ISRAEL! HELP!!! WHY ME??? WHY NOT ME??? You had a real choice here! Give me a bustier, if my nudity offends, but I'm life, baby! I'm the Earth Mama and I *know* what you need! Beat me if you must, I kinda like it, and I know you're wracked with guilt, but DON'T KILL ME!!!!!!! Let *me* be the one, your one and only, I'm here for you, Israel, you alone, oh, baby, hear me, please! PLEASE Hear Me!!! HEAR ME!!!!!!!!!!!! I'M THE ONE . . . LET IT BE ME!!! MEEEEEEEEE EEEEEEE!!!!!!!!!!!! MEEEEEEEEEE!!!!

EEEEEEEEEEEEEEEEEEEEEEEEEEEEEEEEEE!!!!!!!!!!!
HEAR O ISRAEL, THE LORD OUR GOD, THE LORD IS ONE.

AUTHOR'S NOTE

Many of the stories in the Bible were written 800 to 1200 years after the events had taken place, so the stories themselves can be considered commentaries on events. The *midrashim,* commentaries on these commentaries, represent the consuming quest to understand ourselves as Jewish people within the context of our culture. It is this constant attempt to redefine ourselves that seems to exemplify us as a people.

It is interesting to note that our Hebrew God, Yahweh, brought us laws and commandments concurrently with religion, so that our God is clearly a political as well as a religious entity: "He" dictates our morals, ethics, our very way of being. While rereading the story of the golden calf, I was struck by what it means to be a dissenter, the person or thing that defies the established orthodoxy and challenges the political and religious establishment.

Aaron's Rap

by Diane Simkin Demeter

At Mount Hor, near the frontier of Edom, the Lord said to Moses and Aaron, "Aaron shall be gathered to his father's kin. He shall not enter the land which I promised to give the Israelites because over the waters of Meribah you rebelled against my command. Take Aaron and his son Eleazar, and go up Mount Hor. Strip Aaron of his robes and invest Eleazar his son with them, for Aaron shall be taken from you: he shall die there. Moses did as the Lord had commanded him; they went up Mount Hor in sight of the whole community, and Moses stripped Aaron of his robes and invested his son Eleazar with them. There Aaron died on the mountaintop . . .

Num. 20:23–28

Aaron here, Aaron, Yo!
You know, the big brother of the main man Mo'
Aaron, yeah! Aaron, yo!
The one who did the talkin' for my baby bro' Mo'
But I sing my brother, I sing Mo'.
He tell me what to do, and I do it for Mo'
Got my heart, got my head, he say go, I go

'Cause God talked to *him*, didn't talk to me
Said Mo' take the people and walk the sea
Said Mo' up the hill, for the two big stones
Said Mo' you my man, til you a bag of bones
You my man, til you a bag of bones

God talked to Mo, didn't talk to me
Tho' the older brother—a nobody!

Just Mo's helpmate, used to translate
Tell people for Mo'—their fate

Now let's talk about the calf, that golden cow
Weren't my fault, no how, no how
Just followin' orders, that's what I know to do
Who gave me 'em? Well, I forget who
I was just the "yes" man, Aaron, yo!
It wasn't never my gig, it wasn't never my show
It was Mo's glory, I sing his praise
Don't I sing my brother each and every of his days?

But listen up, listen up, I must of took the fall
Who for? Don't know, that's all
Took the fall on Mt. Hor, but who'd I whore for?
Don't know, took the fall for sure, for sure
Mo' stripped me of my robes on Mt. Hor
Stripped me. What for?
I gave that Mo' my all, my all
I think I took the fall

Wasn't Mo' my heart? Wasn't Mo' my head?
He stripped my robes, God killed me dead!

Cain killed Abel, but I loved Mo'
He was my main man, my bro'
Cain killed Abel, but I loved Mo'
My brother Moses,

My baby bro'

Yo!

ADDITIONAL REFERENCES

At this the Lord grew angry with Moses and said, "Have you not a brother, Aaron the Levite? He I know will do all the speaking. He is already on his way out to meet you, and he will be glad indeed, to see you. You shall speak to him and put the words in his mouth; I will help both of you to speak and tell you both what to do. He will do all the speaking to the people for you, he will be the mouthpiece and you will be the god he speaks for.—Ex. 4:14–16

The Lord said to him, "Who is it that gives man speech? Who makes him dumb or deaf? Who makes him clear-sighted or blind? Is it not I, the Lord?—Ex. 4:11

And Moses stretched out his hand over the sea, and the Lord drove the sea away all night with a strong east wind and turned the sea-bed into dry land. The waters were torn apart, and the Israelites went through the sea on dry ground, while the waters made a wall for them to right and to left. —Ex. 14:21–22

The Lord said to Moses, "Come up to Me on the mountain, stay there and let me give you the tablets of stone, the law and the commandment, which I have written down that you may teach them."—Ex. 24:12

AUTHOR'S NOTE

With my baby boomer, 1990's, "hip," psychoanalytic consciousness, rereading the story of Aaron and Moses, I was struck by the fact that the brothers' relationship seemed to be a paradigm of all sibling relationships, and their unexpressed sibling rivalry seemed to be in even greater relief because their "parent" (if God can be conceived of as a parent) was truly omnipotent, not just thought or feared to be so. To continue, if God was parent, was the ultimate voice of compassion and love, but one who had unwavering dictates, who chose favorites and was unforgiving, then the story of the two brothers seemed to reveal a great deal about the power structure of families.

The Daughters of Zelophehad

by Ruth Gilbert

And the Lord spoke unto Moses, saying; "Unto these the land shall be divided for an inheritance according to the number of names . . ." And they that were numbered of them were twenty and three thousand, every male from a month old and upward . . .

Num. 26:52–53, 62

Almost forty years had gone by. The Jews had been wandering in the desert, in the wilderness, all this time. An entire generation of those who left Egypt had died and new generations had been born. Now the people were on the shore of the Jordan River, in the plains of Moab, preparing to cross into the Promised Land. Land promised to them by God nearly forty years before.

It was at this time that God instructed Moses to conduct a second census, for the land would be divided among the descendants of the twelve sons of Jacob. Each individual household would be apportioned land according to its number. In this way the land would be an inheritance to the tribe and the name of each household, each father, would be kept alive by its children.

Zelophehad, was a descendant of Joseph and had died several years before this time. He had five daughters and no sons. When his daughters, who were not married, heard that the land would be divided among the male members of their tribe, but not the females, they were quite distraught. They met on a grassy piece of land on the banks of the Jordan River. There they sat together, silently, each deep in her own thoughts.

Tirzah, the youngest, began to cry. "I miss Father," she said, "If he were still alive he would have an inheritance of land and his name would not be lost." Then Hoglah said, "and what about us? We will have no inheritance at all."

Mahlah, the oldest, looked at her sisters and felt responsible to try to comfort them. She said, "I remember a story that our grandmother told to me. She said the Jewish people were saved because of the righteous women. She told me about the midwives, Shiphrah and Puah who would not kill the first male children born to the Jews as Pharaoh commanded. And about Yocheved, the mother of Moses, who placed her son in the Nile River. And she told me about Miriam who helped to save Moses' life by bringing his Mother to be his nurse."

"I remember a story about Miriam," said Milcah, "it was she who told her father that if the men stayed away from the women not only would sons not be born but there would be no daughters either. And afterwards, when the people were safely through the Red Sea, Miriam took tambourines and cymbals and danced and sang and all the women danced and sang with her."

"Well," said Hoglah, "Do not forget about Miriam's well. It was the well that kept us from thirst as we went through the desert." "Yes," said Noah, "I remember a story also. I remember it was about the women who would not give their jewelry to cast the Golden Calf. And how they tried to stop the men from worshipping that idol at the foot of Mount Sinai."

The five sisters sat on that grassy place on the banks of the Jordan River and they continued to tell stories that they remembered about their foremothers. They talked about their own mother and how she had decided not to marry one of their uncles, for she was too old to have any more children and could not carry on the family name.

Then they talked about what they had experienced while they wandered in the desert. As they spoke, they gained strength from each other. Then they talked about their father and they remembered that he had broken the Sabbath by picking up sticks. They recalled his last words to them, admitting that he knew he had committed a sin and that he was willing to die to teach others to keep the Sabbath holy.

Soon Hoglah, who was the most assertive of the sisters, became restless and said, "We must go to Moses and demand our rights of inheritance so that we can have land and keep our father's name alive."

"Wait," said Noah, the most practical and logical of the sisters. "Wait," she said, "we are all in agreement but let us plan and prepare and wait for the right time and then we will plead our case in front of Moses."

Her sisters agreed with her for they all had faith in God and believed in God's judgment of fairness. Mahlah said, "God's love is not like that of a mortal parent who might show favoritism and speak only of a son. But God, who created the world, gives love to women as well as to men."

And so the sisters waited. They waited for the appropriate day. That day came when Moses was sitting in the tent of study talking to the judges about the law of levirate marriage. The law that said a widow could marry her brother-in-law so that their children would carry on the family name.

On that day the daughters of Zelophehad, who understood the system of judges, went to the lowest judges, the captains of the tens. As the sisters suspected, these judges could only rule on small matters and they were sent to the judges of the fifties. But these judges thought this was too important a decision for them and so the sisters were sent to the judges of the hundreds. "This is too serious a matter for us," they said, and the daughters were taken to the judges of the thousands to present their case. But they, too, deferred the decision to a higher authority.

And so it happened that the daughters of Zelophehad were brought to Moses and stood before him in his tent of study. They began to plead their case with confidence. To show that they were all equal in knowledge and unified in their resolve, each sister presented one argument to Moses.

Mahlah began. "We are our father's only descendants. We stand here in the place of male children. Why should our father's name be forgotten because he had no sons? We ask for an inheritance as you would give to a son."

Hoglah continued. "Our father did not join in the rebellion with Korah who did not have faith in God's commandments. Our father did not go with the people who wanted to return to Egypt."

Milcah spoke next. "Our father's sin was not like that of the ten spies who said we would be eaten as if we were grasshoppers if we went into the promised land of Canaan. Our father did not cause anyone else to sin."

"And remember," said Noah, "Like the women who went before us, we are righteous women who have followed the laws and traditions that have been set down for us."

"Therefore," said Tirzah, "we ask for our father's portion of land and the double portion he is entitled to as a first born, according to the law."

But Moses himself hesitated and finally he said, "I, too, have a superior," and Moses took the question to God. He received the following judgment. "The daughters of Zelophehed speak correctly. What they ask for is in accordance to the laws that I have written. Give them their father's inheritance and two parts of their grandfather's possessions, for their father was his first born."

And so it happened that by this decree their father's name was not lost and the intent of the Torah was fulfilled: land stayed within the family and tribe regardless of gender.

Soon after this decree the daughters of Zelophehad married men from within their own tribe, although they were free to marry whomever they chose. In this way they assured that their land inheritance remained with their tribe.

The daughters of Zelophehad were rewarded. For today, if you travel to Samaria you will find two districts named for two of the daughters, Noah and Hoglah.

ADDITIONAL REFERENCES

And while the children of Israel were in the wilderness, they found a man gathering sticks upon the Sabbath day.—Num. 15:32

And they spread an evil report of the land which they had spied out unto the children of Israel saying, "The land, through which we have passed to spy it out, is a land that eateth up the inhabitants thereof . . ."—Num. 13:32

Now Korah . . . took men; and they rose up in the face of Moses . . . and they assembled themselves together against Moses and against Aaron . . . —Num. 16:1–3

AUTHOR'S NOTE

We know that inheritance is primary in determining who we are, and ownership of land is a mark of wealth and status. Though the daughters of Zelophehad are mentioned several times in different chapters of the Bible, there is no clear explanation of their importance to the laws of inheritance. I wanted their voices to be heard.

As a storyteller, I know that stories can explore feelings and bring life's lessons to us in a comfortable setting. Therefore, *midrash* was a natural form for me to illustrate the importance of equality in land inheritance.

Moses and the Fifth Commandment

by David A. Katz

Moses went up from the steppes of Moab to Mount Nebo . . . and the Lord showed him the whole land. And the Lord said to him, "This is the land of which I swore to Abraham, Isaac, and Jacob, 'I will give it to your offspring.' I have let you see it with your own eyes, but you shall not cross there."

So Moses the servant of the Lord died there, in the land of Moab, at the command of the Lord.

—Deut. 34:1–5

On Mt. Sinai the Lord spoke to Moses saying, "Honor your father and your mother so that you may live long upon the land which the Lord your God is giving you." Then there was a pause; the hand of Moses stopped writing upon the tablet. Moses' heart beat quickly. Could God not know what this commandment meant for him?

Moses cried out upon the mountain, "Dear God, why do You present me with an impossible task? You command us to honor our parents so that we may live long upon the land that You will give us. Yet you know that I never knew my parents. When Pharaoh decreed that newborn Hebrew sons were to be slaughtered my mother placed me in a basket to sail upon the Nile. Though she was allowed to suckle me, as an infant she gave me up to Pharoah's court. My parents gave me life but I never saw them again. I was never able to honor my parents in Egypt and I have no way to honor them now. Do You mean to tell me that because I cannot fulfill this commandment I shall not enter the Promised Land? Am I not Your beloved servant?"

From atop the mountain Moses searched the heavens for an answer . . . but the air was as still as the desert sand. Out of the heavens came silence.

Then anger flared like fire in the heart of Moses. He had grown up in the royal court and had had everything he ever wanted. When his people thirsted under Egypt's sun, he had water. When his people bowed under the hardships of slavery, he sent his hand against the taskmaster. When nobody saw a way to escape Egypt he was the leader who said, "There is no one who can stop us; we can have freedom if we have faith in God." Now it was God who was making it impossible for him to enter the Holy Land. How *could* he honor the parents he never knew?

When Moses descended Sinai and spoke to the people, only Miriam recognized the pain on his face as he recited the fifth commandment. She was his sister and a prophetess too; she knew what he must be thinking. Later, when the people had returned to their tents, she touched her brother's hand and said, "My young brother who talks to God, do not despair. You will learn what the Lord requires of you." But Moses was not comforted and turned away from her.

Years passed and the people wandered through the desert. And the children of Israel continued to cry out. They complained about their food and rebelled against Moses. When they arrived at Kadesh the people began to shout, "Why have you brought the Lord's congregation into this wilderness for us and our beasts to die." And they assembled themselves to strive against him, saying "Why did you make us leave Egypt to bring us to this wretched place, a place with no grain or figs or vines or pomegranates? There is not even water to drink."

Moses faced the people, but he did not respond. He wondered to himself, "Will *I* ever enter the land where grain and figs and vines and pomegranates grow?" Then he thought, perhaps God will answer my prayers if I am the best person I can be and do the right thing by helping my people. He beckoned Aaron, his brother, to support him. Together they approached the Tent of Meeting to speak to God.

"Lord, our people thirst. How can we help them?"

And the Lord spoke to Moses saying, "You and your brother Aaron, take the rod and assemble the community, and before their very eyes, order the rock to yield its water. Thus you shall produce water for them from the rock and provide drink for the congregation and their beasts."

Moses continued, "If I do as you have commanded will you teach me to honor the parents I never knew so that I may enter the Promised Land?"

And God replied, "It is not for you to ask; do exactly what I command for I know what is best for you. You must show me respect for I am the Lord your God who brought you out of Egypt to be your God.

Moses wished he had another God. In frustration and anger he grabbed the rod and stormed from the Tent of Meeting. He ran to the rock God had spoken of; Aaron chased to catch up. Moses turned in fury to the people and shouted to the heavens so God would have no trouble hearing, "Listen you rebels, shall we get water for you out of this rock?" And he raised his hand and struck the rock twice with his rod.

Then God's stern voice came forth from the heavens: "Because you did not trust Me enough to affirm My holiness in the sight of the Israelite people, therefore you shall not lead this congregation into the land that I have given them. These are the Waters of Meribah!"

The words could not have been more clear: ". . . the land that I have given them." Not "you," but "them." It was God's intention that Moses would never enter the Land of Israel.

Soon after these events, the children of Israel ended their journeys through the desert. When the time drew near to part, Moses assembled the people to bless them and bid them farewell. Tears came to his eyes as he spoke to each tribe. First he turned to Reuben, asking God to sustain his tribe though they were few in number. Then he turned to Judah, asking God to protect him. And then he turned to his own tribe, Levi.

But now the words would not come forth. Moses began slowly, struggling, mumbling in phrases only he understood. He spoke of Meribah and of the parents he never saw, brothers and sisters who never recognized each other and children who were never known. He spoke of covenants and laws and things he knew pleased God. He spoke until there were no more words left in him.

Then Moses gathered his strength and finished his blessing. When he was done he ascended Mount Nebo. There he stood, looking across the Jordan River to the Promised Land. His vision was clear, his sight undimmed. There he saw the grain and figs and vines and pomegranates. And when he beheld the great goodness he knew would never be his, he found the answer to his question.

Until this moment Moses had never understood the meaning of a boundary. Now it was time for Moses to learn the lesson which God was teaching . . . that setting boundaries is an act of love, and that accepting limits leads to patience, wisdom and faith.

Moses was now ready to honor the parents he never knew; for he understood that God was loving him, caring for him, teaching him the lessons that parents teach their children.

So Moses listened to the voice of God, accepted the word of God, and honored God that day.

And Moses was silent, and at peace.

ADDITIONAL REFERENCES

—Honor thy father and thy mother. Ex. 20:12
—Birth of Moses. Ex. 2:1–10
—At the waters of Meribah. Num. 20:1–13
—The final blessing of Moses. Deut. 33:1–11

AUTHOR'S NOTE

When God commands Moses to speak to a stone in order to bring forth water, Moses hits it instead and therefore is not permitted to enter the Promised Land. For centuries, commentators have tried to explain why God would punish Moses so harshly for such a seemingly small infraction. Perhaps the answer lies in the very nature of boundaries.

Rosh Hashanah

The Ram at Moriah

by Peter Lovenheim

*And the angel of the Lord called unto him out of heaven, and
said: "Abraham, Abraham" . . .*

*And Abraham lifted up his eyes, and looked, and behold
behind him a ram caught in the thicket by his horns. And
Abraham went and took the ram, and offered him up for a
burnt-offering in the stead of his son.*

—Gen. 22:11, 13

One day, in the land of Moriah, a ram with great curled horns
grazed alone at the foot of a mountain. He was a strong ram, and
wise, a leader of his herd. As he was pulling at some choice tufts of
grass, God called to him.

"Ram," said God.

"Here I am," answered the ram.

"At the top of this mountain," said God, "near where a man
and a boy are beginning to build an altar, there are some bushes. I
want you to climb up there now and catch your horns in them."

The ram laughed.

"God," he said, "I've roamed these hills all my life. I know every
rock and crevice and bush for miles around. Asking me to catch
my horns in a thicket is like asking a fish to drown or a bird to
forget how to fly."

"This is important," said God. "I need your help right away."

Curious now, the ram asked God what the problem was.

"I have asked the man Abraham to prove his faith by offering his
son Isaac as a sacrifice," God explained. "But the boy must not be
harmed. That is not what I intended. Isaac must live; it is important
for all mankind. I need you to be the sacrifice in his place."

The ram thought a moment.

"God," he said, "You know I would do anything to help. But I've had plenty of experience with human beings, and I'm not so sure I want to sacrifice my life for them. We animals do a lot for them, but for the most part they are selfish and ungrateful."

"I know what you mean," said God.

"For example," said the ram, "my brother the ox treads out the corn, but human beings muzzle him so he can't eat even a single mouthful."

"You are right," said God. "I will forbid human beings to muzzle the ox while threshing."

"And my brother the mule," continued the ram, "is willing to pull the plough, but when humans yoke him together with stronger and faster animals, it nearly breaks his back to keep up."

"I will forbid human beings to yoke to the plough two animals of different species," said God.

"And then, after all that hard labor," said the ram, "when do working animals ever get a chance to rest?"

"All creatures should rest," said God. "I will tell human beings to rest their animals on the Sabbath."

God thanked the ram for bringing attention to these matters.

"Ram," God asked, "now will you help Me by climbing the mountain and catching your horns in the thicket?"

"But there is another matter," said the ram. "Isn't it enough that animals do hard labor for human beings? Must they also kill us for food? We have no peace, and the pain is unbearable."

"In the Garden," said God, "I showed people how to nourish themselves without killing. They can still do so if they choose. But I cannot make the choice for them. Still, the animals should not be made to suffer; I will instruct the humans how to slaughter with the least pain."

Now all the time God was talking to the ram at the foot of the mountain, God was also keeping watch on Abraham and Isaac at the top.

"Ram," said God, "you must climb the mountain. Time is running short."

"But there are other cruelties," protested the ram. "The hunter, the trapper, the tanner . . ."

"Isaac is bound to the altar," said God. "Time is short. I cannot make rules for every case. You know I have mercy for all the creatures I have made. I will tell all humanity that those who would be righteous must respect the lives of their animals."

Satisfied, the ram began to climb the mountain. But just short of the top, he stopped.

"God," he called, "how long must we be put to the fire for the sake of Your name?"

"Not long," said God. "In time, man will honor Me more with deeds than with smoke and fire. The sacrifices will stop."

"Now hurry," said God. "Abraham lifts the knife."

The ram raced to the mountain top and spotted the thicket of bushes. Just beyond, he could see Abraham standing before the altar, his gleaming knife held high above Isaac's chest. Quickly, the ram lowered his great, curled horns into the thicket and, in an instant, on the back of his neck, felt the gentle touch of an angel's hand.

ADDITIONAL REFERENCES

Thou shalt not muzzle an ox when he treadeth out the corn.—Deut. 25:4

Thou shalt not plow with an ox and an ass together.—Deut. 22:10

. . . the seventh day is a sabbath . . . in it thou shalt not do any manner of work, thou, nor thy son, nor thy daughter, not thy man-servant, nor thy maid-servant, nor thy cattle . . . —Ex. 20:10

Behold, I have given you every herb yielding seed . . . and every tree . . . to you it shall be for food.—Gen. 1:29

Thou shalt kill of thy herd and of thy flock . . . as I have commanded thee.—Deut. 12:21

The Lord is good to all. His tender mercies are over all His works.—Ps. 145:9

The righteous man regards the life of his beast.—Prov. 12:10

To what purpose is the multitude of your sacrifices unto Me? saith the Lord: I am full of the burnt-offerings of rams, and the fat of fed beasts . . . —Isa. 1:11

AUTHOR'S NOTE

As a boy, I was always intrigued by the role of the ram in the story of the binding of Isaac; the ram seemed an innocent victim of the drama being played out between Abraham and God. Later, I studied the many biblical injunctions against cruelty to animals and was puzzled over how to reconcile these humane laws with what still seemed unfair victimization of the ram. But what if the ram were not a victim? What if the ram knew exactly what it was doing and, in the biblical tradition, had bargained with God on behalf of its kind? The ram would be ennobled, then, no longer a victim.

Yom Kippur

The First Yom Kippur

by Howard Addison

And God spoke to Moses after the death of Aaron's two sons . . . with that Aaron will come to the holy place . . .
—Lev. 16:1, 3

What was it like on the first Yom Kippur?

Aaron was up all night before. He was so excited that he couldn't sleep a wink. He wanted to make sure that he would be ready at dawn, when the service was scheduled to begin. He knew that everything depended on him tomorrow, and so he was nervous.

As he lay in bed, recollections of the past year kept going through his mind. What a year it had been!

"We confronted Pharaoh, Moses and I, and we won. We crossed the Red Sea, and we saw Pharaoh and his army drown there. We stood at Sinai, and we heard the Voice that gave us the Law there. What a day that was! I'll never forget it."

And then Aaron stopped short. His face turned pale. The grin on his face gave way to an expression of guilt, as he remembered what happened afterwards.

"Moses went up the mountain and left me in charge. Forty days went by, forty long days, and Moses didn't come back. He was late for some reason—who knows why? And the people panicked. They thought he was never going to come back, and they were scared. They didn't know what they would do without him. Some wanted to turn around and go back to Egypt; others wanted to go forward without Moses; and some wanted to have a golden calf that would take the place of Moses. They ganged up on me from all sides:

'Aaron—What are we going to do?'

'Aaron—we've got no leader. He's never gonna come back.'

145

'Aaron—build us a calf!'

"I tried, I tried to stall them, but I couldn't. They wouldn't listen. They were in a frenzy. They would have killed me if I didn't agree to do it. So finally I gave in. LESS THAN SIX WEEKS BEFORE, God had said: "You shall make no graven images," and now I made a golden calf for them!

"I did it. And I was so ashamed afterwards. When Moses came down the mountain and saw what had happened, he was furious— at them and at me. And when he said to me, "Aaron, how could you do such a thing?" I didn't know what to say. I just hung my head in shame. I was so mortified, so embarrassed!

But he forgave me. He gave me a second chance. He let me stay on as *Kohen Gadol* and even made a fancy Installation Ceremony for me. And what a day that was! There was pomp and circum- stance, and a parade.

And then Aaron thought about what had happened on that day, and as he did, his heart overflowed with grief, and tears came to his eyes. For that was the day when his glory turned ashes. In the middle of the installation, his two sons, Nadav and Avihu, both died. No one is quite sure how it happened.

"How could it have happened? How could I have LET it hap- pen? People had tried to warn me. They had tried to tell me. They had told me that my children were playing around with drugs and that they were drinking. But I didn't pay attention. I didn't believe it. I didn't want to believe it.

"It was my fault. I should have talked to them. I should have listened to them. But I was too busy with communal affairs. I had meetings every night. There were the ritual committee, the school committee, the youth commission—and now it is too late. Now they're gone . . ."

And Aaron sank into the depths of pain and self-flagellation and grief and remorse. But he was awakened from his reverie by the voices of his two remaining children:

"Dad," called Elazar, "It's dawn!"

"Father," called Itamar, "The rites are about to begin. The people are waiting."

Aaron stirred himself and got out of bed. He put on his golden garments, which he had laid out the night before. And then he shook his head. "No, this isn't the right thing to wear today. Gold reminds God of the sin of the golden calf." He took off the golden garments and put on a plain, simple, white linen robe instead. And he went out to perform the ritual.

As he stepped out of his tent, he saw that a great crowd of people had come out to cheer him on. How good of them to come. They must know how nervous he felt, and had come out to encourage him.

He started walking down the road towards the altar, and as he did, he looked at the crowd. There was Ginsberg. He hadn't seen Ginsberg at a service in a long time. He was surprised to see him there today. Ginsberg had lost two of his children during this past year. They had been stricken with one of those rare tropical diseases that afflict people in this wilderness of Sinai. And since that happened, Ginsberg had not come to services, not even once. Aaron knew what he felt like, for he, too, had lost two children this past year. When it happened, Aaron remembered, he had been unable to talk, unable to pray, unable to officiate at the services for a long time, until finally Moses was able to get him to come back and lead the services again. He knew what Ginsberg was going through because he had gone through it himself, and so he reached over the rope that the police had set up to keep the crowd in order and shook Ginsberg's hand. He could feel Ginsberg's hand tremble, and he could see the pain in his eyes. He pressed his hand a bit harder, as if to say: I know how you feel, and he whispered, "Thank you for coming," and then he went back to the procession.

A little further on, he saw Greenberg. What was he doing here? He hadn't spoken to Greenberg ever since the incident of the golden calf. Greenberg was one of the leaders who had pushed him into doing what he did that day, and there were many nights since then that he lay awake cursing Greenberg for what he had done. But now, as he passed him, he realized that Greenberg had come out to wish him well on his mission, and the anger inside him melted. So, as he passed him, he reached out over the crowd and patted him on the shoulder, as if to say: "It's okay. I understand what you did. You meant well. You did it because you were scared."

Greenberg looked startled when he touched him, and then a smile of relief came onto his face, and the anxiety and guilt in his

eyes faded. "Thanks," he said to Aaron. "Thanks a lot. I appreciate that."

All along the way, Aaron saw familiar faces. There was Levy,
who had tried to calm the mob that day and keep them from
making the golden calf. Levy had been badly beaten. He was in the
infirmary for weeks afterwards, and some of the scars and bruises
were still visible on his face and arms, but he was there. Aaron
gave Levy a thumbs-up signal as he passed him. And Levy winked
back and gave him the high sign.

And so it went all the way. He saw the Feinsteins, who had
rebelled against God when they ran out of food and water, and
he knew how they felt for he, too, had rebelled against God
and lost faith for a while. He saw the Finkelsteins, who had lost
a son in the war against Amalek, and he remembered how he
had tried to comfort them, and how inadequate and inept he had
felt that day. He couldn't think of anything wise to say to them. All
he could do was sit with them and listen to them lament over and
over again for hours, just as he had when he lost his own children.
How good it was for them to come out and cheer him on today. He
must remember to send them a thank-you note when the day
was over.

Then he arrived at the altar. There, he cast lots between the
two animals that waited for him. On one, he put all the sins of the
Jewish people, and that one he drove off into the wilderness as a
scapegoat. Why do people need scapegoats? he wondered. Why
do they insist on putting the blame for what they do onto someone
or something else? I don't know, he said to himself, but that's the
way it has always been, and I guess that's the way it will always be.
On the other animal, he put all the sins of the sanctuary. He knew
that the sanctuary had sinned too, had sinned many times during
the year. He know that the holier something was, the more liable to
corruption it was. He knew how often during the year the sanctuary had been a place of petty politics; how often the Levites had
quarreled over who would get which honor, or who would go first
in the procession, or who would get the solo part in the choir
pieces. He knew how often people came there just to be seen, how
many sins had been committed there, by him and by others. So he

sacrificed an animal to atone for the sins of the sanctuary, and put its blood upon the horns of the altar.

And then he went into the Holy of Holies. By the time he got inside he was emotionally exhausted. So many people he had seen along the way! So many that he didn't think cared about him, had come. So many people that he cared about more than he realized, had been there!

All he could say when he got inside was, "*Ribono shel olam,* I know we have done many wrong things in this past year, but please be patient with us, and give us a new chance and a new beginning. Take care of Levy, would you please, and let his bruises heal. Forgive Greenberg for what he did. He was scared, and people do all kinds of things when they are scared. Help Ginsberg and his wife, please, and help the Feinsteins and the Finkelsteins too. They seem so down, so discouraged.

"And help me and my wife too, God. Help us raise our two children that we still have left. May we do better with them than we did with the other two. May we spend more time with them, and may they turn out right.

"And please help all the Jewish people, God. We make mistakes, I know we do. We've made a lot of them this year. But please forgive us and give us a new year. If you do, we'll try to do better this time."

By the time he finished saying these few words, his eyes were damp. All the fancy words that he had intended to say when he got inside were forgotten. But as he walked out of the Holy of Holies, he felt cleansed and rejuvenated and fresh again. He felt better than he had in many months.

And so that night Aaron held a party for all his friends, to celebrate the new year. Moses came, and Levy came, and Ginsberg and Feinstein and Finkelstein and Greenberg and all the others, and his children were there too. They helped him host and helped him clean up afterwards. And when the party was over, he and his wife and children hugged each other and wished each other well, and said to each other: "We hope that it will be a good year for you this year, a better year than last year."

And God said: *"Amen."*

AUTHOR'S NOTE

1983 was a most painful year. The conclusion of an eleven-year marriage, the suicide of a friend who was also president of my *schul,* the death of my brother. Two years prior to these events, I had read Henri Nouwen's *The Wounded Healer.* His claim that Christianity saw Jesus' power to heal as coming from his wounds, sparked my thinking about Aaron's role in Judaism for us. As Yom Kippur 1984 came closer, I became even more captivated by Aaron, the wounded healer of Israel. I decided to tell his story, hoping that, in some part, it could become my own.

An Heretical Jonah:
A Midrashic Fantasia

by Menorah Lafayette-Lebovics Rotenberg

"And should I not care about . . . that great city, in which there are more than a hundred and twenty thousand persons who do not yet know their right hand from their left, and many beasts as well!"

—Jonah 4:11

This is a story about Yonah ben Amittai: Jonah the son of Amittai, a believer in God and God's truth *(emet)*. Jonah had also been a true believer in "the Lord, the God of Heaven, who made the sea and land." and he had worshipped God until his thirteenth summer, the summer of the "great fish" *(dag gadol)*. The events of that summer were to leave him with his soul seared and his belief shattered.

Jonah was the youngest of his many brothers and sisters. As often happens in large and bustling families, the youngest, Jonah, was the family favorite. He was a sunny, equable and engaging child. Left to his own devices a great deal of time, he roamed the countryside and grew up a lover of plants and of animals. As he grew older, he began spending more and more time with his brothers who were shepherding his father's flocks. Amittai, Jonah's father, felt this was a good choice for him. Jonah would make a good shepherd. He was caring about the animals entrusted to him and sensitive and imaginative enough to deal with the solitary life imposed on the shepherd. So Jonah began his apprenticeship and preparation for adult life.

Then one day, an extraordinary thing happened. A merchant happened by. That in itself was not extraordinary but this was a special traveler, for he was a seafaring merchant and such men did not often pass through the hilly countryside of Gat-Hepher where Jonah lived. As the traveler told his tales, Jonah's eyes sparkled and his cheeks flushed. Jonah could already imagine himself astride a great sea beast urging it on to greater speeds, diving down to the depths, and then just as he could no longer hold his breath, hurtling up to the surface again. Such were Jonah's fantasies even as he listened to the traveler's more mundane stories.

Jonah's intense listening and yearning looks were not lost on the merchant, for he had young children of his own. He recognized Jonah to be a very special child, and so he did an extraordinary thing. One night he said to Amittai, "I would like to take Jonah back home with me—to Joppa—for the summer. I have seen the wonder in his eyes and know that even more wondrous imaginings are stirring within him. I will take him, and return him safely."

Jonah held his breath to await his father's decision. Amittai looked at Jonah, his favorite, beloved child. Then Amittai looked at his wife, Amit. Should they let their youngest and dearest son go with this man? Who was this seafarer? Why had he come into their life? And who was Jonah? For it was not only the sea merchant who had recognized the specialness of Jonah; his parents had known it a long time as well, but it had never been told to them that their son was to be a prophet. And then amidst all these questionings—or perhaps, despite them—the decision was made. Perhaps the decision had been made from old. Jonah would go "down to Joppa."

Jonah and the merchant arose early in the morning and went down to Joppa, down to the sea that Jonah had never seen. The sea and the surf and the reefs were all beyond anything he had imagined. Just as he had gotten to know the animals and plants of his countryside, he plunged in and the sea became home to him. There were no great beasts to ride astride but there were deep dives down to the sea floor where he would gaze at the stunning sea animals. The exotic, iridescent colors and flashing sparkle of their luminous skins were beyond description. Truly God's handiwork was incredible and wonderful to behold. All through the summer Jonah swam and dived with the sea creatures. He wove garlands of weeds and twined them about his head, dived down deep to the base of the reefs and imagined what it would be like to be a sea horse. That summer, Jonah was the most joyful and thankful he had ever been in his thirteen years.

And then one hot sultry day, with the east wind blowing so strong as to be almost suffocating, the awful thing happened. It began early in the morning. Jonah was awakened by sounds of shouting and general bedlam. He jumped out of bed, tugged on his clothes and followed the shouting down to the sea shore. There on the beach was a sight Jonah was never to forget as long as he lived. Stretched across the shore was a white, unbelievably huge sea beast. People were exclaiming that it must be a leviathan, or a behemoth, or some incredible beast of old. In the end, they called it simply, *dag gadol* (huge fish) or *ha-dagah* (the female fish). What to call it, however, was less a problem than what to do about it. It was clear that the *dagah* was already beginning to suffer.

Slowly some chain of command was formed with Jonah's sea merchant designated the head. A plan was developed to get the *dagah* back into the sea. It was no easy task, nor did they think it would be. As graceful and self-sufficient as the *dagah* was in the sea, she was equally cumbersome and dependent on land. In the sea, despite its weight of 150 short tons, it could frolic and cavort with ease. But on the shore it could barely move. Instead, it lay prostrate heaving its enormous bulk. Hundreds of townsmen were deployed to relay buckets of water to wet the length of the great fish (95 feet long).

Meanwhile, a raft of sorts was being built, onto which the *dagah* was to be moved and then hauled back into the sea. Some of the children tried to get the great fish to drink and eat; Jonah was the one to try most often. He would stroke the *dagah,* wipe its incredibly enormous brow with the wet sponge he kept near him, and urge her to take some nourishment. He would croon and sing to her as he had with his father's sickly sheep. At times he thought the great fish looked at him thankfully with its big soft eyes, and Jonah's insides quivered.

After what seemed an eternity, the raft was ready and the men were gathered to transfer the great fish onto it. After another eternity, and another day, the great fish had been transferred and hundreds of boats were readied to pull her out to the depths of the sea. And when it was time, by now the third day, the ropes were cut and the *dagah* could again swim in the sea. Jonah went down with her as far as he could and whispered farewell. He wanted this fairest and most marvelous of creatures to know how much he loved her and that he would remember her always.

Jonah went back with the boats to the shore, to the large thanksgiving feasts that were being prepared in honor of God's deliverance of the great fish. And when the feasting and thanksgiving were over, the townspeople returned to their well-deserved rest.

It seemed to Jonah that he had barely been sleeping when he was roughly roused by his friend, the merchant. "Come, Jonah, the *dagah* has returned. We will mobilize and return her again." This time, however, the Herculean effort was less well attended and in contrast to the first effort, grumbling was heard from some quarters. Yet few were prepared to desist and see the magnificent beast perish. After a very long time, the *dagah* was again returned to the sea.

Once again Jonah accompanied his beloved white fish. But Jonah was deeply troubled. He wondered whether his love for the *dagah* had seduced her into returning to the shore. He was horrified to think that love could have murderous consequences, to think that something that felt so good could have such a devastating effect. So this time, in parting from his *dagah,* he did not tell her of his love for her. Rather he enjoined her not to return. He told her that the sea creatures and the land dwellers from time immemorial had lived side by side but not together. He reminded her that God "made both sea and land" and that in doing so, he had separated them forever. This separation was at times tormenting and one could choose not to accept it. But to be together sowed its own seeds of sorrow and painful consequences. Jonah hoped the great fish understood. He was letting her go, for his love for her was great and sure, and not murderous. Jonah said farewell to his *dagah* and this time, after she left, he wept.

This time when the boats returned to the shore, there was thanksgiving but no feasting. The townspeople were weary and there was trepidation in the air. As before, everyone returned to rest, but Jonah slept fitfully. Nor was he surprised to hear the merchant enter his room, crying out as he roused him, "A great misfortune has befallen us, the *dagah* has returned a third time. Come Jonah, let us call upon God. Perhaps God will be kind to us and she will not perish." Jonah understood from this that there would be no rescue attempted again. So Jonah went down to the seashore to find his beloved great white fish. Tears welled from his eyes, his throat was choked, and his insides were constricting. Jonah was furious, and uncomprehending. How could the *dagah* persist in her wayward course? For as the prophet Jeremiah said: "Even the stork in the sky knows her seasons, And the turtledove, swift and crane keep the time of their coming . . ." Twice she had beached herself and twice she had been rescued. Jonah could not fathom this aberrant behavior. He could understand that humankind might remove itself out from the Law, but God's other creatures were not endowed with perversity. Therefore, for God's other creatures, God's Law had to work perfectly. And if there came a time when that Law seemed deficient—or that God's creatures acted deficiently—Jonah expected God's intercession to right the aberration.

So Jonah prayed, ". . . I know that You are a compassionate and gracious God, slow to anger, abounding in kindness, renouncing punishment." But when God's intercession was not forthcoming, Jonah gave the *dagah* what comfort he could while he waited for her death. And when she died, Jonah cried out, "Please Lord, take my life, for I would rather die than live." The Lord replied, "Are you that deeply grieved?"

Jonah was deeply grieved and continued to mourn the death of his great fish and the ways of God. His friend the sea merchant, brought him home to his family safely, as he had promised Jonah's father. On the surface, he seemed changed, but not so completely that he stood apart from his adolescent peers who were also undergoing many changes.

But Jonah was haunted by visions he could not share. He could not communicate the devastating effect of his encounter with the *dagah* and became estranged from those close to him. He remained a caring shepherd, but gaiety had gone out from him forever. For gaiety comes from knowing that God is good. What happened to his *dagah* was a subversion of God's goodness. Jonah was but in his thirteenth year and had no way of handling his horror. He continued to shepherd for his father and remained in his father's home.

So time passed. Jonah became the master shepherd. He was adored by his young apprentices because he cared not only for the sheep but for them as well. Yet neither they, nor anyone else could get to know him well. More and more he became a solitary man sunk in profound and disturbing thoughts. From time to time, Jonah wondered idly about the future. While he did not actively seek death, he did not think he would avoid it if it came his way. With the passage of time, healing had not taken place, and life seemed increasingly empty and futile.

And then one day, into this empty landscape of his life: "The word of the Lord came to Jonah, son of Amittai: "Go at once to Nineveh, that great city, and proclaim judgment upon it; for their wickedness has come before Me." Jonah's reaction was immediate. "He started out to flee from the Lord's service." Jonah called on God not to send him. He told God that he was a shattered vessel and would not be able to hold any divine words. But God held firm. It was God's intention to show Jonah that disaster was not always the way of the world. Indeed, God had not interceded for Jonah's great white fish, but now he would intercede for a whole city "in which there are more than a hundred and twenty thousand persons who do not yet know their right hand from their left and many beasts as well *(uveheymah rabah)."*

When the Ninevites returned from their evil ways, God would forgive them. God hoped that Jonah would then be reconciled to divine ways, forgive God and allow healing to take place. If Jonah were to return, it would have to be with God's help. *"Hashiveynu, Adonai eylekha—ve-nashuvah"* (Turn us back O Lord to Yourself— and we will return. God knew it was necessary to restore the illusion of goodness to Jonah. *"kadeysh yameynu k'kedem"* (Renew our days as of old!). God had all the props prepared, the fish had been ready and waiting in the wings since the Creation. God held firm.

And so, Jonah began to pack for his journey. He did not have much to pack save some goods and some money. He began his journey, a brooding man haunted by his visions. He walked steadily, looking neither to the right nor to the left. And for the second time in his life, Jonah "went down to Joppa, and found a sea vessel going to Tarshish." With the money he had packed, "he paid the fare and went aboard with the others to Tarshish, *away* from the service of the Lord . . . But the Lord cast a mighty wind upon the sea . . . and the ship was in danger of breaking up." The captain went to find Jonah, who had gone down to the depths of the ship to find peace and sleep. The captain roused him crying: "Up, call upon your god! Perhaps the god will be kind to us and we will not perish."

Jonah, however, was indifferent. In another time, and what seemed to be another age, he had uttered just such a prayer—and it had not been responded to. So the sailors cast lots and the lot fell on Jonah. They said to him: "Tell us, you who have brought this misfortune upon us, what is your business? Where have you come from? What is your country, and of what people are you?" And Jonah replied: "I am a Hebrew" and he added, "I worship the Lord, the God of Heaven who made both sea and land." For Jonah had no difficulty in acknowledging God's sovereignty. His quarrel was not that God ruled but God had not interceded. And the sailors were terrified and asked Jonah what he had done. And when they learned he was fleeing from the Lord's service, they asked him, "What must we do to you to make the sea calm around us?" And so now the question Jonah had often pondered while tending his father's sheep was his to answer. He had not sought death, nor would he avoid it. Perhaps he could be rid of his loneliness, of the emptiness he carried within him, lo these many dreary years. And so he did not hesitate long before he answered. "Heave me overboard for I know that this terrible storm came upon you on my account." "And they heaved Jonah overboard, and the sea stopped raging."

As Jonah pitched into the water, he thought he saw a brilliant huge streak of white float by. Then, suddenly, there was only darkness, and a dreamlike rocking sensation. And when his "life was ebbing away" Jonah "remembered the Lord." God was aghast. This was not the return *(teshuvah)* that had been planned. God wanted Jonah to be restored to reality despite the pain of reality so "The Lord commanded the fish, and it spewed Jonah out upon dry land."

And "the word of the Lord came to Jonah a second time: "Go at once to Nineveh, that great city, and proclaim to it what I tell you." And this time, Jonah no longer called out to God. Nor did he try to flee God's service. After sleepwalking through his adult life, he had summoned his last bit of energy to flirt with death. He had pitted himself against God—unsuccessfully. Now if God still wished to use a shattered vessel Jonah would protest no more.

So Jonah "went at once to Nineveh" and proclaimed: "Forty days more and Nineveh shall be overthrown." Now "the people of Nineveh believed God." They were evil, yet they had belief. They believed that if everyone turned back from evil ways, "who knows but that God may *turn (yashuv)* and relent? He may turn back from His wrath, so that we do not perish."

While Jonah was waiting to see what happened to the city, he left and found a place east of Nineveh. And God brought out the various props he had provisioned for this very occasion. "The Lord provided a *kikayon* plant—to provide shade for his head. . . . But the next day at dawn, God provided a worm which attacked the plant, so that it withered. And when the sun rose, God provided a sultry east wind; the sun beat down on Jonah's head, and he became faint."

Now Jonah remembered the sultry suffocatingly hot day. This is how it had been the day of "the coming of the great fish." He became faint and his memories became unbearable. He begged for death saying, "I would rather *die* than live." Then God said to Jonah: "Are you so deeply grieved about the plant?" "Yes," he replied tonelessly, "so deeply that *I want to die.*" And Jonah knew that God knew it was not the plant that Jonah was referring to.

But what could be done at this point? The *dagah* had died long ago and God had not interceded. That could not be be undone. Could Jonah not recognize, however, the enormity of what God was prepared to do *now?!* He was prepared to renounce the punishment God had prepared to bring upon Nineveh "an enormously large city." Not since Sodom and Gomorra was God prepared to show the vastness of his merciful qualities—based not on justice nor on Nineveh's proven evil track record, but on Divine compassion and graciousness. Nineveh promised it would *turn* from evil. God asked only for the intent before extending deliverance.

God did not know of any other way to have an impact on Jonah. Even now God hoped to impress him, crying out to Jonah with passion: "And should I not care about Nineveh, that great city, in which there are more than a hundred and twenty thousand persons who do not yet know their right hand from their left, and *many beasts* as well *(uveheymah rabbah)*."

Now Jonah smiled. He was amazed that he was truly happy about Nineveh's salvation. God's caring and compassion *had* reached him and warmed him. He came to understand that life could be lived joyfully.

But withal, Jonah recognized that a basic fault line lay at the very core of his being. He knew he lacked redemptive belief, having learned too early in life that—in a blink of an eye—terrible and unimaginable things can happen that can never be undone.

So while God had spared Nineveh, for Jonah and his great beast *(uveheymah rabbah)* God's deliverance had come too late.

ADDITIONAL REFERENCES

God said, "Let the water below the sky be gathered into one area, that the dry land may appear." And it was so. God called the dry land Earth, and the gathering of waters He called Seas. And God saw that this was good—Gen. 1:9–10

Even the stork in the sky knows her seasons,
And the turtledove, swift, and crane
Keep the time of their coming;
But My people pay no heed
to the law of the Lord.—Jer. 8:7

Take us back, O Lord, to Yourself,
And let us come back;
Renew our days as of old!—Lam. 5:21

"I am a Hebrew," he replied. "I worship the LORD, the God of Heaven, who made both sea and land." JONAH 1:9

It was he who restored the territory of Israel from Lebo-hamath to the sea of the Arabah, in accordance with the promise that the LORD, the God of Israel, had made through

His servant, the prophet Jonah son of Amittai from Gath-hepher. II KINGS 14:25

Jonah, however, started out to flee to Tarshish from the LORD's service. He went down to Joppa and found a ship going to Tarshish. He paid the fare and went abroad to sail with the others to Tarshish, away from the service of the LORD. JONAH 1:3

The LORD provided a huge fish to swallow Jonah; and Jonah remained in the fish's belly three days and three nights. Jonah prayed to the LORD his God from the belly of the fish. JONAH 2:1–2

The captain went over to him and cried out, "How can you be sleeping so soundly! Up, call upon your god! Perhaps the god will be kind to us and we will not perish." JONAH 1:6

He prayed to the LORD, saying, "O LORD! Isn't this just what I said when I was still in my own country? That is why I fled beforehand to Tarshish. For I know that You are a compassionate and gracious God, slow to anger, abounding in kindness, renouncing punishment. JONAH 4:2

Please, LORD, take my life, for I would rather die than live." The LORD replied, "Are you that deeply grieved?" JONAH 4:3–4

Gone is the joy of our hearts;
Our dancing is turned into mourning. LAMENTATIONS 5:15

The word of the LORD came to Jonah a son of Amittai: Go at once to Nineveh, that great city, and proclaim judgment upon it; for their wickedness has come before Me. JONAH 1:1–2

And should not I care about Nineveh, that great city in which there are more than a hundred and twenty thousand persons who do not yet know their right hand from their left, and many beasts as well." JONAH 4:11

Who knows but that God may turn and relent? He may turn back from His wrath, so that we do not perish." God saw what they did, how they were turning back from their evil ways. And God renounced the punishment He had planned to bring upon them, and did not carry it out. JONAH 3:9–10

But the LORD cast a mighty wind upon the sea, and such a great tempest came upon the sea that the ship was in danger of breaking up. JONAH 1:4

They said to him, "Tell us, you who have brought this misfortune upon us, what is your business? Where have you come from? What is your country, and of what people are you?" JONAH 1:8

He answered, "Heave me overboard, and the sea will calm down for you; for I know that this terrible storm came upon you on my account." JONAH 1:12

And they heaved Jonah overboard, and the sea stopped raging. JONAH 1:15

When my life was ebbing away,
I called the LORD to mind;
And my prayer came before You,
Into Your holy Temple. JONAH 2:8

The LORD provided a huge fish to swallow Jonah; and Jonah remained in the fish's belly three days and three nights. JONAH 2:1

"Go at once to Nineveh, that great city, and proclaim to it what I tell you." JONAH 3:2

Jonah started out and made his way into the city the distance of one day's walk, and proclaimed: "Forty days more, and Nineveh shall be overthrown!" JONAH 3:4

The people of Nineveh believed God. They proclaimed a fast, and great and small alike put on sackcloth. JONAH 3:5

The LORD God provided a ricinus plant, which grew up over Jonah, to provide shade for his head and save him from discomfort. Jonah was very happy about the plant. JONAH 4:6

And when the sun rose, God provided a sultry east wind; the sun beat down on Jonah's head, and he became faint. He begged for death, saying, "I would rather die than live." Then God said to Jonah, "Are you so deeply grieved about the plant?" "Yes," he replied, "so deeply that I want to die." JONAH 4:8–9

Jonah went at once to Nineveh in accordance with the LORD's command. JONAH 3:3

AUTHOR'S NOTE

My ideas for this *midrash* came to me from conscious and subconscious thinking. Consciously, I was intrigued by Jonah's need to flee the burden of prophecy. I wondered what cataclysmic occurrence had shattered his ability to believe in the possibility of deliverance.

The subconscious shapers of this *midrash* are as follows: Early intermittent separations from my mother destroyed my trust in the basic goodness of the world. The death of our first and still-born daughter, strangled by the very cord created to sustain her, became the model for the *dagah* cavorting in glee in her amniotic waters.

The spectral image of the Holocaust is never far from my consciousness. Despite the emergence of the State of Israel, God's deliverance came too late for those who perished, for those who were sent to "the left or the right" (cf. Jon. 4:11).

Sukkot

Pillar of Cloud

Debra B. Darvick

And the Lord went before them by day in a pillar of cloud, to lead them the way, and by night in a pillar of fire, to give light to them; to go by day and by night.

—Ex. 13:21

"Come, Rachel," Batya said, handing Rachel a long and sturdy stick. "Beat this rug with me. If we don't clean the sand from it soon, it won't be much different from the Exodous, when we walked ankle deep in the desert sand!" Batya had hung the rug on the outside wall of the temporary hut, the *sukkah,* that was her home during her peoples' gathering days. Rachel took the stick from the old woman and set to the task. Batya's arm was strong and solid; her rug-slaps sent great clouds of dust into the air. Rachel sent only whispers of sandy dirt from the rug's woven threads, but she worked with determination beside the older woman. They were silent, save for a cough now and then as the dust escaped from the rug. At last, brilliant reds and blues gleamed from Batya's rug.

"I'd forgotten how pretty this was," Rachel said, laying her stick upon the ground, brushing sand from her palms. "You can't really see the dust, but it's there just the same." With her finger, she began tracing the rug's threaded patterns. "Is that what God looked like, Batya?" Rachel asked. "Like the clouds of dust from the rug?"

Batya knew where Rachel's mind had wandered. As one of the few remaining elders who could tell about the Hebrews' terrifying liberation from Egypt, Batya was asked every now and then to retell the miraculous journey.

"Now there's a story," she said easing herself down beside Rachel. "Yes, God did travel before us in a cloud; but it wasn't like a cloud of rug dust or even like a cloud in the sky. Mind you, I was a child during that hard journey away from Egypt, but I remember thinking I had never seen anything so tall.

"The pillar that was God stretched so high into the sky that my neck hurt whenever I tried to see the top. And it changed. Each time I looked at it, I saw something different swirling within. Most of the elders thought it was only a cloud of dust, but if you looked through the dust you could see all kinds of things. My friend Dina and I saw animals one minute, plants and trees the next. And the faces! Some were very beautiful. Others were angry and frightening. Some were children's faces and others were of people so old we thought they must be dead!

"When it was too hot to walk during the day, we walked at night. The pillar changed from cloud into a great column of fire. And just as the cloud held dozens of things to look at during the day, the images in the fire changed constantly too. That pillar blazed like the hot sun yet sometimes it was cool and quiet as moonlight. One time it looked like cooking fires and another time, it sparkled like the mischief in your brother's eye. And sometimes, there was so much to look at that Dina and I had to turn away. The fire was too powerful, the faces and animals were too much for us to stare at for very long.

"And you must also remember, we were not always close enough to see anything at all. The women and children were often the furthest behind and then, we could only see the pillar's outline way ahead of us. But it was always there, guiding us by cloud and fire for forty years. As I got older, I saw the images less and less often. Perhaps a child's eyes are better at seeing things like that, or perhaps I got so used to seeing it that it was no longer remarkable."

"Do you miss not being able to see God, Batya?" Rachel asked. "How can you know something is there when you can't see it?"

"That's an old, old question," Batya replied. "Let me tell you a story my mother once told me. Long ago in Egypt, there was a man who could never work fast enough to please Pharaoh's captains. So one day a captain hit him on the head and blinded him.

"Even though he was blind, his hearing was very sharp; he knew who was near him by listening to the sound of approaching footsteps. He could tell the hour of the day by the feel of sunlight on his face; he knew birds by their calls and could tell that dusk was coming just by feeling for the coolness of the night air. Sight isn't always the most important way of knowing something.

"I think it is like that with God. God is in the love your mother has for you and in the sound of the birds that call out each day. God is in the pattern of the stars and in the shape of the palm branches. And maybe God is even like the dust in this rug.

"Remember when we began, you said you didn't know how much dust was hidden in the rug until we started working. Our eyes aren't always the best way to see things. Perhaps it's like that with God. We have to work before we can see God, too.

"Now come," Batya said leaning on her stick to stand up, gesturing towards the *sukkah*. "You take one side and I'll take the other and we'll put this clean rug back inside."

AUTHOR'S NOTE

In reading the text of Exodus I was captivated by the image of God as a pillar of cloud and fire. Being able to call to mind a picture of God is a challenge, especially when talking to children. The figure of an old man with a hoary beard is so limiting!

I have always leaned to the Chasidic view that sparks of God's essence are all about us; we have merely to open our eyes. I think it is important to make God's presence as accessible as possible for our children. Let's tell them that a morsel of God's energy is in the leaf that was green yesterday and is red today even as we talk about chlorophyll. If our children have a connection to the divine as youngsters, they will be able to grapple with the idea of God as they mature.

Simchat Torah

The Dreams of the Torah

by Rosie Rosenzweig

" . . . on the eighth day you shall observe a sacred occasion
and bring an offering by fire to the Lord . . ."

Lev. 23:36

She was awakened from a happy dream as hands pulled her from
her resting place. Protected by the golden oak doors, quieted by the
heavy and woven wool curtains picturing the flaming *Alef-Bet* letters, and lying quietly under a skylight open to the gently swaying
acacia trees, she had been enveloped in her favorite reverie.

The reverie was more than a dream; it was really a memory or
perhaps a flashback to that time before her first creation, before
her introduction into the material world. Before flesh, before
bones, before growing things, she had been the fire dancing with
the Holy One, only herself and the One. This was before the
descent, the painful constricting descent, to be trapped in forms,
with skin and bark and earth, when the holy sparks were caught
and hidden within form. The mission in this world was to find
these sparks again.

This jolt from the reverie was like that first jolt centuries before
when the Holy One of Commandments, commanded the Torah to
leave and descend into the material world. The Torah resisted so,
in the beginning, that the Holy One allowed her to keep her fire
and appear as the fiery *Aleph-Bet* letters dancing. It was the
descent into the tablets that was the first pain, the first pain of
forming. At this moment, amid the vibrations of the *Shofar's* song,
the Torah understood the pain of childbirth. It was only the soothing shine of Moses' face that comforted the Torah; Moses' face
shone with the closeness to the Holy One.

Then Moses raged with anger at the first sight of the Golden Calf. Swift like the wind, the Torah's stone vessel was broken and gladly she flew back to the Holy One's side.

Like the first creation, failure ruled in the world of sentient beings.

The second descent taught the Torah to bear more pain; like a mother at the birth of each subsequent child, she learned the mission of this pain. The guidance of Moshe Reibeinu helped her through the years of wandering in the desert. The shine of Moses' face soothed her. The tender voice of the Holy One spoke from between the two golden angels of the Tabernacle. To the Torah it was a vibration of warmth and comfort.

The Torah was forever thankful for the bright spaces between the blackness of her letters. The spaces reminded her of her earlier state when she was just pure fire. Even without ears she could resonate with singing voices. When the soul of the singer was being raised up on the ladder of her golden notes, the Torah could touch the Holy One of Love again, and then just for an instant.

Now, in this wooden barn, the Torah had been jolted again; obediently she fell into outstretched hands. This was a yearly ritual, this dancing about; this was the ultimate pain for the Torah, the hands of this world, the containment, the adjustment to each embrace, and the vibrations from the drums and the musicians. She was thankful for the velvet covering, the soft protection from the many hands.

Slowly she girded herself to stand the world of people: the men's dance, the women's dance, and most painfully, the children's dance. The feel of the music was like a continuous earthquake as the children groped, and clung and fell. Because she had no ears she could hear no music. She was only conscious of the vibrations in the sanctuary, the way the floor shook, the clutch of some who danced with her, and the caress of others.

During the children's dance she felt the sweaty hands of the smallest, the eager short steps of her bearer. The Torah felt jolted and wished that this dance would end.

Finally the dancing stopped. She felt the vibrations of hushed voices around her. From previous years she knew what was to

come: the disrobing of her velvet dress and the cold empty air—
even worse, the unrolling to expose her core of vulnerability.

They unrolled her and unrolled her and unrolled her, until
every letter from B'reshit to Vezot Ha'Brakha was open for all to
see. No more piecemeal presentations as at every Shabbat reading. Here was the whole story from beginning to end. Only when
the beginning and the end touched for one moment, did the Torah
feel safe in the circle of the unending letters.

At this moment the Torah remembered when her letters were
fire in the Holy Time of Creation—and everytime they sparked fire
after that: when Akiva lighted the crowns of the kingly letters,
when they danced around the martyrs who were wrapped in the
flaming scrolls, when Abulafia meditated on them in Safed, when
the Marahal of Prague summoned them to create a Golem and
withdrew them to draw life from Golem, when the Kotzker Rebbe
heard the pure prayer of the peasant reciting the *Aleph-Bet* but
above all, when they were magically suspended in the tablets
during Moses' descent from Sinai. They could always spark fire.

So when a little child, barely thirteen, began to read the first
words, the Torah knew the voice belonged to one of the young
people who had grasped her during the children's dance. As those
first words were being sung, the Torah recognized the spark of
pure fire in the reader's eyes.

And the Torah was happy again to be one with the One.

AUTHOR'S NOTE

Midrash is a very poetic form, and the source of poetry is the
very heart of mysticism. To write in these forms is sometimes a
very meditative act, and, for me, a form of prayer. This midrash,
on how the Torah entered the manifest world, was inspired by
the way Congregation Beth El in Sudbury celebrates Simchat
Torah: the congregation opens the entire Torah into a circle
with the ends touching, and in sections, studies each Torah
portion and summarizes it. I often wondered how the Torah felt
at these moments.

Tu Bi-Shevat

Tu Bi-Shevat

The First Kippah

by Lawrence E. Kurlandsky

The earth brought forth vegetation: seed-bearing plants of every kind, and trees of every kind bearing fruit with the seed in it. And God saw that this was good. And there was evening and there was morning, a third day.

God said, "Let there be lights in the expanse of the sky to separate day from night; they shall serve as signs for the set times—the days and the years; and they shall serve as lights in the expanse of the sky to shine upon the earth." And it was so.

—Gen. 1: 12-15

As Shana pressed her face to the frosted window, she knew that her life would never be the same. Hillel had come home today, on Tu Bi-Shevat. The setting sun stained the sky the color of strawberry ice cream, which then began to melt over the snow-covered land. The birthday of the trees. It was hard to believe. The pine trees were dressed for the occasion with their white crowns and white robes draping their green everyday clothes. The leafy trees were stark naked except for the modest old oak, which kept a girdle of dried leaves around its middle. Only the excited rustling of the parade-ready regiments of cornstalks standing shoulder to shoulder hinted at the gaiety of the day.

"Hillel, my new baby brother," Shana thought, "well, not really new." She remembered the first time she had seen him. "It had been days, weeks, months ago. Dad told me that Mom had had a baby, but it was hard to tell if he was happy or sad. Then Dad said that the baby had to stay in a place called a hospital because he had been born too early. Eventually, I got to visit. The hospital was sort of like . . . a zoo, a petting zoo really. Each baby was in a plastic cage, and there were yucky tubes and things every-where. Not to be mean or anything, Hillel had looked more like a baby chipmunk than a baby boy. After that, we went to visit Hillel often. Although my Mom and Dad always seemed a little worried, it was fun. While mom and dad got to hold Hillel, the nurses talked to me and gave me cookies and juice. They were nice to me even when they had so much to do. Visiting my baby brother in a zoo and then going home with Mom and Dad was great. Then one day, they told me that Hillel would be coming home soon. They both looked so happy; I couldn't believe it. I threw myself on the floor and began to kick and scream. But of course, it has not changed anything. And so today, the Birthday of the Trees, had been the day."

Feeling the warmth of the fireplace on her back, Shana turned from the window and her gaze alighted upon her grandparents seated around the fire. Her attention was drawn to Grandma Sarah who was crocheting *kippot* in preparation for Hillel's upcoming *brit*. Shana loved to watch Grandma's fingers. So quick, fine, and sure were their movements as they turned a ball of yarn into a colorful kippah.

Shana asked, "Why do people wear *kippahs?*"

Grandpa Yosef and Grandpa Shmuel looked up and said that a *kippah* is a sign of respect for God, to remind us that God is above and always present.

Grandma Brindl Chaya, who had been sitting quietly by the fire, said, "Shana, come over and sit on my lap and, I will tell you about the first *kippah*." This is the story she told.

"It was the Fourth Day. God had just created the Sun. With a great flourish, a brilliant ball illuminated the Earth. The creation of the Sun was witnessed by the trees and plants that had been created the day before. On that Third Day, they had groped in the dark with their limbs and roots seeking other signs of life. But now on the Fourth Day, their eyes had been dazzled by the sunlight. As they grew more accustomed to the light, evergreen trees began to stretch toward the sky. Deciduous trees, created without leaves, began to leaf out. Some, embarrassed at their nakedness, first blushed with pink or white flowers before they could cover themselves with leaves. As each tree beheld its neighbor, it could only marvel at the variety of leaves around it. Many trees were bejewelled with fruits of every possible color.

As the Fourth Day wore on, a few trees began to sense that something was wrong, but feared to say anything lest it spoil the festive air about them. Slowly this sense of foreboding spread. Finally even the ascetic acacia knew that something was seriously wrong. Leaves turned brown and withered. Sap, the life blood of trees, began to boil and bleed from the branches and trunks. Panic spread among the trees. The problem became clear to all: the sunlight was too powerful! The very light they had welcomed that morning, which had warmed their faces and caused them to flourish, was now going to be the cause of their death.

From around the Earth, a council of trees was called to meet immediately. The council decided that God must be approached by one of them. But which tree should be their spokesman? After much discussion, the White Pine was chosen—its trunk so stately and tall; its branches so protectingly long, stretching upward to the heavens as though in prayer and supplication; its needles a blue-green to remind God of the Earth's pleasing colors; and its needles so caressingly soft. Surely God would see that this tree came in peace and not in anger.

And so, as the Fourth Day came to its end and newly created moonlight bathed the Earth, the White Pine addressed God. "My Creator, I come in peace to speak to You of life and death matters. The Sun, Your most wondrous creation today, is too powerful for the trees on Earth. If You do not help us, we will all die. Please consider taming the sun's awesome energy."

As the trees had feared, God was angered by these words. "How dare you, tree, you whom I have given life, criticize the Sun, a most wondrous creation. Perhaps I should destroy you and all your ungrateful friends now as you stand there before Me."

But the council of trees had chosen their spokesman well. As the soothing voice of the White Pine came forth from its whispering branches, God's heart was softened. God saw how lovely was this magnificent work of Creation as the tree stood bathed in the silver light of the moon. And God thought, "I am tirnd. The work of four continuous days of creation are beginning to take their toll. As infinite as My powers and mind are, I have never before undertaken an act of Creation of this magnitude. Everything has been planned down to the smallest detail. But has it?" For but a sliver of eternity, doubt entered the mind of God. "What if I have overlooked something? There is so much still to do. My finest acts of Creation are yet to come. I cannot turn back now. But what if this tree is right? Perhaps all My future Creations are endangered or doomed?"

The infinite composure of God returned, and God was reassured of the goodness of Creation while taking the measure of this White Pine. As the tree stood quietly waiting, God addressed it. "White Pine, you are indeed one of the good and great acts of My Creation. You have the potential to do good things. My work is of an infinitely complex design. My plans for tomorrow and the next day are too full. There can be no changes. I trust in you and your good friends to find a way to save yourselves. You may return to your home in peace with My goodwill and blessing."

Grateful for this meeting and thankful to be alive, the pine bowed and bid God goodnight. But the pine was stunned. "I have failed. How can I face my friends and report that God will do nothing?" As the pine traveled along, it sensed that it was no longer the same as when it had started the day. It had been in the presence of God, and the memory, like a fine perfume, was intoxicating. God had said that they could find an answer. So the tree thought and thought, and slowly an idea began to take shape.

Upon its arrival back at the council of trees, the White Pine said, "I have spoken with God. This is what we must do. We will gather all the trees on Earth. Each of us gives off special vapors. We will weave these together into a canopy which will shield us from the full force of the sun's rays." Word was sent, and all the trees joined in the task. With great care, a fine invisible tapestry of vapors was woven together high above the Earth. When completed, it covered the Earth better than a *kippah* covers a bald man's head. The trees, tired and hopeful, awaited the Fifth Day of Creation.

When that Day dawned, an intact veil hung over the Earth finer than the finest silk and more valuable than if spun from gold thread.

The trees rejoiced as they felt the life-giving warmth of the sun but not its deadly searing rays, and they danced in the wind. God too, saw what the trees had done and saw that it was good. With a smile, a lightened heart and step, and renewed strength, God completed Creation in Six Days and rested on the Seventh Day."

Grandma Brindl Chaya paused here to sip some tea, but then she went on as Shana got more comfortable in her lap. "I believe that when God sees a *kippah,* God is reminded of the first *kippah* and remembers the role that the trees played in Creation to make it even better. We, too, owe much to the trees for their miraculous fragile veil. Tu Bi-Shevat allows us to say thanks to the trees and remember to plant new ones so that the Earth's *kippah* will always remain over us.

"In Israel, Tu Bi-Shevat comes just before the spring. On that day, each tree relives the Fifth Day of Creation when their lives hung in the balance, wondering if the right conditions would come about for them to survive. And so each spring, trees wonder whether the right conditions will come together for a good year. It is fitting that Hillel came home on this day. His life, too, hung in the balance. Through the actions of doctors and nurses, God's creations, he was able to come home to us.

"To me, little Shana, the *kippah* is a reminder that each of us is a part of God's Creation and has the ability to accomplish great good in this world. We may not yet know what it is, and perhaps neither does God. But as the White Pine has shown both God and us, this may be the surest measure of God's infinite wisdom and goodness. Well Shana, it's time for you to go to bed."

With a bigger smile than when she had started this day, Shana gave everybody a big hug and kiss. As she skipped off to bed, she thought, "Maybe good can come even from a baby brother."

AUTHOR'S NOTE

Why did God create trees before sunshine? Why is there a hole in the Earth's ozone layer? Why was my son born prematurely? Why was it Tu Bi-Shevat when we were able to bring him home from the nursery? Stirring thése questions all together cooked up this story.

This midrash is told through the person of my mother, Bernice, who introduced me to the wonders of storytelling as a child. She died the day after this manuscript was accepted.

Purim

Vashti

by Susan Terris

*What shall we do unto the Queen Vashti according to law,
forasmuch as she hath not done the bidding of the king
Ahasuerus by the chamberlains?*

—Est. 1:15

It was a time of mead and revelry,
a time when my husband's mantle purpled
the earth from India to Ethiopia
as did legends of my beauty.
Still, Hadassah, whom you know
as Esther, is all you ever hear about,
because on the seventh day
of one last wild feast
when my husband was mad with wine
and called for me, I did not come.
Like a cow or an ass, like a piece of
rich tapestry, he valued me:

a thing to be appraised and appreciated
by drunken guests.
He wanted them to ogle gold,
silver, shell, cords of fine linen,
tiles of onyx marble
along with my ankles, my teeth,
my firm white breasts.
I was but property, my refusal to comply
a sin. Besides, he was afraid
other women would take
courage and rebel.

So, by the law of Persians and Medes,
he cast me out penniless,
decreeing sanctimoniously that now:
*all the wives will give to their husbands
honor, both great and small.*

An interesting decree, one which
rationalized his too-predictable search
for a fresher, younger wife
to take my place. And he chose
another smart, willful woman
who dared to disobey him.
In her case, history brought
glory, renown, vindication; in mine
only obscurity.
Still, I would like to think, Hadassah
drew sparks of
her courage from the ashes of mine.

AUTHOR'S NOTE

Most biblical stories need interpretation or commentary of one sort or another. Therefore, midrash seems to be a natural response to reading them. I chose the Book of Esther because I've always been drawn to Esther and Ruth as the only two biblical women to merit having a book of the Bible named after them. I've identified with Vashti ever since I was chosen to portray her (because I was tall, dark-haired, and assertive) in some long-ago Purim pageant in which the girl chosen to be Esther was small, fair-haired, and compliant.

Passover

Pesach Death, Pesach Demands

by Adam Fisher

. . . the Lord struck down all the first-born in the land of Egypt . . .

—Ex. 12:29

The Lord spoke . . . "Consecrate Me every first-born; man and beast, the first issue of every womb among the Israelites is Mine."

—Ex. 13:1–2

While we celebrated,
ate the Pesach lamb,
God killed first-born Egyptians.
We heard
cries in the village,
sobbing mothers, screaming fathers.
Some stopped eating
grew quiet.
Soon we heard people run
frantically toward us,
so we hid from yet another pogrom—
this one (or so we thought) for revenge,
but they demanded, "Leave now!"
We grabbed what we could,
began to run in joyous panic.
Some saw their fear,
demanded jewelry and clothes.

A few refused
to accept.
Later, God told us,
"Separate out
your first-born
for Me."

ADDITIONAL REFERENCES

And Pharoah . . . said . . . "Up, depart from among my people . . ."—Ex. 12.30–31

The Israelites . . . borrowed from the Egyptians objects of silver and gold, and clothing.—Ex.12:35

Exodus Meditation

by Adam Fisher

With Pharaoh chasing them
the sea a barrier
Israel's children ask,
"What have you done to us,
taking us out of Egypt . . .
where we sat
by fleshpots?"

—Ex. 14.10–11; 16.3

Our children raised
with camel races
and game shows after work;
strangers without memory of Jacob,
or yearning for holiness.
How do they learn
the Unseen One leads us?
How do we answer
when this journey
is what we are,
not something to be explained?

Pesach

by Adam Fisher

". . . the Israelites had marched through the sea on dry ground, the waters forming a wall for them on their right and on their left."

(Ex. 14.29)

Israel fleeing
past the dead
in pyramidal tombs
they built,
fleeing the humbled god Pharaoh;
forced through the narrow canal of sea,
after salt water breaks:
New-born
children of God.

AUTHOR'S NOTE

In each of these poems (as in all midrashim), a point in the text sparks a thought that resonates within me.

In "Pesach Deaths/Pesach Demands," the close approximation between the verse telling us that God killed the first-born Egyptians and the verse in which God demands the first-born of the Israelites, struck me with its symmetry.

"Exodus Meditation" tries to imagine the parallel between those at the time of the Exodus who did not understand the significance of what they experienced and those of our time who are alienated from their heritage. This poem previously appeared in the *CCAR Journal* (Winter, 1986).

"Pesach" builds on the birth imagery in the text. This poem previously appeared in *The Reconstructionist* (April–May, 1986).

Shavuot

The Silent Journey: A Story of the Passage of Naomi and Ruth

by Rachel Havrelock

And Ruth said: Entreat me not to leave thee, and to return from following after thee; for whither thou goest, I will go; and where thou lodgest, I will lodge; thy people shall be my people, and thy God my God.

Ruth 1:16

Day 1: Where You Go, I Will Go

A life of tents was never expected of me. As a girl, I never learned this particular art. It was my husband Mahlon who taught me. Before his death, I often accompanied Mahlon and his flocks to the wilderness of Moab. If we got lost in the darkness, Mahlon would reassure me with laughter. He would say, "We are safe. I am a Hebrew destined for a life of wandering and tents." Strange that it was a Hebrew who taught me the terrain of my native land. He taught me what to eat in the wilderness, how to make alliances with things unseen, how to negotiate paths.

Yet on the path I traveled away from Moab, it was not Mahlon whom I walked with but his mother, Naomi. Both of our husbands were dead and Naomi was determined to return to her native town of Bethlehem. How could I let an old woman travel alone?

So I joined her in a return to a place I knew only through stories. Part of me expected Naomi to have this path mapped out in her memory and to navigate with the great Hebrew instinct. But I soon realized that Naomi was depending on me to lead her back to her home.

We didn't walk far that first day. We covered a few miles in silence and then stopped in the wilderness of Moab. It had been a long time since I had set a tent. Naomi sat on a rock and watched me as I raised the sticks and cloth. Perhaps it had been a long time since she had seen a tent rising—since her husband Elimelech had first brought her to Moab.

I never knew Elimelech or much about him. Mahlon had refused to talk about him. "What's there to know? He fled our home in Bethlehem during times of famine and brought us here." And if I asked Mahlon how Elimelech had died, he would say, "From the disease of here."

I had wanted to ask Naomi these questions that my husband would never answer. So while I set the tent, I did. But when I questioned the cause of Elimelech's death, Naomi turned her face from me and would not answer. From that moment on, I knew that we had an agreement to never speak the name of the dead. So "the disease of here" was all I was ever to know of Elimelech's end.

Wrapped in dusk, we sat outside the tent. I busied myself by counting stars and giving them funny names. Naomi rocked herself back and forth whispering, "your people are my people; your God my God; where you die, I will die; and there I will be buried." These words were mine. Yet each time I caught a piece of her whispering, it had a different meaning to me than when I had said the words myself. I thought, perhaps Naomi will one day give these words to other women as a song, perhaps they will be passed down from generation to generation, perhaps my words will live forever.

When we lay inside the tent, Naomi finally spoke words that were not my own. "I am returning like the wanton children of Israel after slavery. But you Ruth, you are a traveler as Abraham was a traveler." Then, I swear, I heard the old woman giggle. I thought to ask her why she giggled, but I understood her words to be pieces of a larger puzzle.

Day 2: The Wind in the Palms

When I woke, Naomi's eyes were lifted toward the sun. "Ruth, you must learn to rise early, when the sun faces you like a lover. If you sleep too long, the sun will meet you face to face like an enemy." I turned my face toward hers and she turned hers toward mine. "Mother," I said, "I have heard that the water of the Salt Sea soothes the muscles. I would like to be soothed before we continue." "So we go," she said as she rose.

I had laid eyes on the Salt Sea only once before, but had floated there many times in dreams. As we walked toward the sea, I remembered a dream. *I was floating in the sea alone. The only sound was the sound of my legs splashing the water until a voice called out to me, "Ruth, are you listening?" "Who is there," I asked. "El Shaddai," was the voice's answer. When I looked around me, I saw no one there. I was still alone but I no longer felt alone.*

When the sun was highest and facing us like an enemy, we stopped for shade and drink by a spring. Cupping water in her palms, Naomi said, "I cannot cross the water tonight." "We are safe," I replied, "we will camp next to the water and cross tomorrow." I didn't know where I was going, but I hoped my reassurance would keep Mahlon's voice alive and comfort Naomi.

It grew dark as we moved toward the Salt Sea. Even in blackness, the air felt thick and hot. We were lucky that some light breezes cut through the heat and cooled us. I felt an alliance with the wind, for it traveled as I was traveling. With this wind sweeping across the desert, I first understood what I was doing. I was leaving behind both of the lives that I had known earlier: the life of a daughter and the life of a wife.

True, I had married a foreign Hebrew. But to me, this was not unusual. I grew up listening to my father's tales of the wandering Hebrews. As a girl, I would wake at the sound of his sandals moving across the courtyard and run to him. He would lean down to stroke my head and look at me with eyes made wild by the fire.

"Have you come for your story, you little beggar?" he would tease. Then he would sit me on his knee and begin, "And it was in those days of long ago." He told many kinds of stories, but we both favored the tales of the Hebrews and their invisible God.

When the young Mahlon first came to tea at our house, my father clapped his hands and said, "I always knew it would be a Hebrew." So I left my father's house and went to Mahlon's. How different this departure from that one. That time, I was transferred from father's hands to Mahlon's and exchanged for some sheep. It was I who chose this path.

The wind in the palms brought me back to the night, to the half moon and the stars. Naomi and I walked until we came to a flat hilltop. "The night is so warm that we do not have to raise a tent," I told her. We lay down blankets and I thanked the winds before falling asleep.

Day 3: The Mikvah in the Jordan

Naomi sat at the edge of the hilltop, holding her legs in her hands like a basket. I followed her line of vision to the sea, which glowed before us in the morning sun. "Sweet waters of the Jordan, you travel to this place and become bitter and undrinkable. My life, my life was once so sweet," Naomi seemed to say to the sea. I rose from the blankets and held her in my arms. She rested her uncovered head on my shoulder. I saw the toll of the desert in her hair, the miles of dust, the tangles of sleeping in a tent and not using oils.

"Look at us," I said, "Let's get in that Salt Sea and have it make us beautiful."

"The sea is not as you expect."

I smiled. "I like surprises."

We gathered our things and went down to the shore. I stood, startled when Naomi began to take off all of her clothes. "Ruth, it is allowed. Women often come to bathe in the Salt Sea." I made no move to undress until she assured me several times that this was permissible. I started laughing when I took off all my clothes and didn't stop until Naomi and I were immersed in the water and realized that we couldn't sink. We floated on our backs and raised our legs high in the air. We bobbed up and down, waved our hands wildly, and kept laughing. I paddled away from Naomi and looked to the sky. "El Shaddai, are you with me?" I asked. And I knew that the answer was "Yes."

When we got out of the water, the sun was already high, and our bodies were covered in the oils of the sea. "Naomi, I don't want to put on my skirt and robes, my body's so oily." "Don't worry, when we cross the Jordan the oils will wash away," she said. I understood then that after crossing the river, we would be in the legendary land of the Hebrews.

We followed the bank of the Salt Sea to its opening where the Jordan River feeds it. The river was rushing past us. Naomi explained that the river was swollen; it was the beginning of the barley harvest.

Standing before the river, I felt a sadness come over me. Would I ever cross this river again? I prepared to look behind me and take one last gaze toward the fields of Moab, but Naomi grabbed hold of my neck. "Do not look back," she said. "Now there is no looking back. Once, a woman turned to salt for that." I remembered my father's story about the wife who turned her face toward the blazing cities and became a pillar of salt. So I looked ahead to the golden hills stretching before me.

I took Naomi's hand. "I am ready," I told her. We set our feet on the rocks of the Jordan until we felt only water and then swam until we felt rocks again. As we crossed, I felt the oil of the Salt Sea, the dust of the road, the sadness of Mahlon's death, and my life in the fields fall away into the water.

Day 4: The Road to Ephrath

Neither of us could rest that night, so we began the ascent from the Jordan River Valley up the Judean Hills. As we climbed the steepest hill, I asked, "El Shaddai, are you with me?" "She is with you," Naomi answered.

In the light of morning, Naomi's excitement became apparent. She began to speak rapidly. "By the afternoon, we will be in Bethlehem. It is harvest time so the fields will be bursting with life. Bethlehem is a place of happiness. My home. We're so close. We just need to follow the road."

"Naomi, will they recognize you?"

"They will remember me," she answered.

When the road began to flatten, Naomi turned to me. "You are tired, my daughter, we will rest at the tomb of Rachel." In the shade of some palms by Rachel's grave, Naomi told me of the great love shared by Rachel and Jacob and how Rachel's father tricked Jacob by giving him the eldest daughter and making him work seven more years for Rachel. She told me of Rachel's barrenness and how she finally gave birth to a famous dreamer. Naomi explained how Rachel left her home on the other side of the Jordan to follow Jacob to his land. "Rachel was strong like you," Naomi said, "she did not make it to Bethlehem, but you will."

I made my own promise to the spirit of Rachel that I would complete her journey and make it to Bethlehem. Then I looked at Naomi and made another promise to myself to take care of her. A bedouin woman approached and gave us water to drink. She gave me a long look and a smile. "Bethlehem," she said pointing down the road. "My Bethlehem," Naomi said to me. I wondered what Naomi's people would think about her returning with a Moabite in place of her husband and sons. After drinking, Naomi stood up, faced Bethlehem and said, "I am ready." She took my hand and we walked the rest of the way to the city gates.

AUTHOR'S NOTE

In *midrash,* the biblical oral tradition is alive and well. We are still telling the same stories and still wrestling with the same concepts. We create *midrash* to wrestle with these ideas on our own terms. *Midrash* represents our dialogue with biblical storytellers and our ability to debate their view of the world. In *midrash,* ideologies new and old collide and influence each other in a dynamic process of narrative evolution.

Four years ago, when Professor Mishael Caspi first asked me to work with him on a book based on the story of Ruth, I secretly groaned. "Isn't that the book with the woman in the fields who gets down on her knees in front of a man?" I asked him. He advised me to spend some time with the story and then to answer my own question. Since then, my question and my answer have changed many times. The story of Ruth has become inseparable from my own life's journey. I bring Ruth and Naomi with me down San Francisco city streets and up the mountains of Northern California. They have taken me across the Jordan River and to the fields of Bethlehem where a woman can walk in full independence.

Biographical Information

HOWARD ADDISON is the rabbi of Temple Beth Israel, Sunrise, Florida, and a teacher of Jewish mysticism at Florida International University. An essayist and former magazine columnist, Addison is the author of *Shutafo: Partners with God*. He has contributed to *Emet V'Emunah, The Seminary at 100* and *The World of the High Holy Days*.

ROBERT B. BARR, ordained from the Hebrew Union College-Jewish Institute of Religion in 1981, is the Founding Rabbi of Congregation Beth Adam in Cincinnati, Ohio. Barr is committed to creating Jewish literature and liturgy that give a humanistic expression to Judaism.

PHILIP COHEN Teaches Judaic Studies at the University of Massachusetts and is the rabbi of Congregation Or Atid in Wayland, Massachusetts. He is currently at work writing a collection of original midrashim focusing particularly on relations between men.

DEBRA B. DARVICK has had work appear in the *Detroit Free Press,* the *Dallas Morning News,* the *Cleveland Plain Dealer,* and the *Chicago Tribune.* She writes for the *Jewish Parent Connection* and is a regular columnist for the Jewish *Women's Journal.* She lives in Birmingham, Michigan, with her husband and son and daughter.

DIANE SIMKIN DEMETER is a writer currently residing in San Diego, California. Among other works, she has written *Frankie and Annie,* a play produced at the Manhattan Theatre Club in New York City. In addition, she has written mini-operettas for the television program *Saturday Night Live.*

RABBI MARLA J. FELDMAN is Director of the Jewish Community Relations Committee of Delaware. She was ordained from Hebrew Union College–Jewish Institute of Religion (New York) in 1985 and obtained her JD from the University of Florida, College of Law, in 1993. Her modern *midrashim* and other articles have appeared in several publications.

PAMELA S. FELDMAN-HILL is a professional artist specializing in Judaic art. She has an MA from Ohio State University. Her paintings and *ketubot* are exhibited and collected throughout the country. She is also a teacher, writer and lecturer. Feldman-Hill lives in Columbus, Ohio, with her husband Greg and daughter Libby.

ADAM FISHER is a poet who has been published widely in journals and magazines. His two books of poems are: *Rooms, Airy Rooms,* and *Dancing Alone. Seder Tu Bishevat,* and *An Everlasting Name: A Service for Remembering the Shoah* are his liturgical works. Among his prizes is an Anna D. Rosenberg award for poems on the Jewish experience (1991). Fisher was ordained in 1967 and received a DHL (majoring in *midrash*) in 1971, both at Hebrew Union College-Jewish Institute of Religion. He has served Temple Isaiah, Stony Brook, New York, since 1971.

MARC GELLMAN, Ph.D., is the rabbi of Temple Beth Torah, Melville, New York. In 1989, Harper & Row published a collection of his *midrashim* for children entitled, *Does God Have A Big Toe?* and illustrated by Oscar de Mejo. In 1991, he published with his friend Monsignor Thomas Hartman, *Where Does God Live?* which won the 1991 Christopher Award.

RUTH GILBERT is a library media specialist and professional storyteller. She has had several articles published in professional journals and enjoys telling stories to "children of all ages." Gilbert believes that stories help us understand our present and lead us toward our future.

JOEL LURIE GRISHAVER is the Creative Chair of Torah Aura Productions and the Alef Design Group as well as an instructor at the University of Judaism and the Los Angeles Hebrew High School. He is the author of *40 Things You Can Do to Save the Jewish People,* and more than fifty other books.

SUSAN GROSS is a freelance writer, mother of two daughters, and synagogue volunteer. Her work has appeared in such publications as *Lilith: The Independent Jewish Women's Magazine, Matrix Women's Newsmagazine,* and *Taking The Fruit: Modern Women's Tales of the Bible.*

RACHEL HAVRELOCK is a renegade scholar and co-author of *In the Mothers' Footsteps: Ruth and Naomi on the Biblical Road.* She lectures and gives workshops on biblical journeys and ecofeminism and the Bible. Havrelock lives in San Francisco, where she writes, translates, and swims in the Bay.

BARBARA D. HOLENDER is a poet. She is author of *Ladies of Genesis* (New York: Jewish Women's Resource Center, 1991), where her poems in this volume first appeared, and also *Shiva Poems: Poems of Mourning* (Newington, CT: Andrew Mountain Press, 1992). Her work has been included in numerous journals and anthologies, including *Sarah's Daughters Sing,* ed. Henry Wenkart (Hoboken: Ktav Press, 1990), *Taking the Fruit,* ed. Jane Sprague Zones (San Diego: Woman's Institute for Continuing Jewish Education, 1989), and *Lifecycles: Jewish Women on Life Passages & Personal Milestones,* ed. Rabbi Debra Orenstein (Woodstock, VT: Jewish Lights, 1994). Her third book of poems *Is This the Way to Athens?* will be published by the Quarterly Review of Literature in its QRL Contemporary Poetry Series.

DAVID A. KATZ is the rabbi of Temple Israel, Staten Island, New York. He received his BS and MA degrees in Speech/Theatre at Northwestern University. At Hebrew Union College–Jewish Institute of Religion, he earned an MA in Hebrew Education and an MA in Hebrew Letters before being ordained in 1981, in New York City. He is a Reform Jewish Educator (RJE) and has written extensively in the areas of Jewish education and liturgy.

MARGARET KAUFMAN, poet and fiction writer, leads writing workshops in Marin County, California, and serves as poetry coordinator for the Napa Writers Conference. A long poem, "Sarah's Sacrifice," was set as a cantata by Ben Steinberg. *Aunt Sallie's Lament* is her most recent book. "Lot's Wife" first appeared in *Ploughshares* (Spring 1994).

LAWRENCE E. KURLANDSKY is the kindergarten teacher at Congregation Ahavas Israel in Grand Rapids, Michigan. In his spare time, he's a pediatric pulmonologist and pediatric-clerkship teacher for medical students. A child at heart, his favorite medium is storytelling.

MARTIN LEVY is a rabbi and poet residing in Kingwood, Texas. He is the spiritual leader of Temple Beth Torah. His work has appeared in the *New York Times* and numerous magazines. He received an award from the 1993 Rosenberg Poetry Competition.

Rabbi Levy was a competitive figure skater, and currently competes in adult dance championships.

LISA LIPKIN is a professional storyteller, writing and performing original works. She has performed throughout the United States and abroad, including appearances on television and radio. Her works have appeared in a variety of publications including *The New Yorker, The New York Times,* and the *Jewish Forward.* She has received fellowships from the New Jersey State Council on the Arts, The New Jersey Historical Commission and the Arad Arts Project in Israel.

PETER LOVENHEIM is a writer and a lawyer. He received his law degree from Cornell Law School in 1978. His articles on Jewish and consumer issues have appeared in *The New York Times, New York* magazine, *Moment,* and *The International Jewish Monthly.* His *midrash,* "The Ram at Moriah," was first published in 1985 in *Genesis 2.* Lovenheim is also author of two books on dispute resolution, *Mediate, Don't Litigate* (New York: McGraw-Hill, 1989) and *How to Mediate Your Dispute* (Berkeley, CA: Nolo Press, 1996).

ALLEN S. MALLER is the rabbi at Temple Akiba in Culver City, California. He is the author of "God, Sex and Kabbalah," and editor of *Tikunay Nefashot,* a contemporary, spiritual, High Holiday prayer book.

RAFE MARTIN is an award-winning, internationally known author and storyteller. He has performed and spoken throughout the United States and as far away as Japan. His work has been featured in *Time, Newsweek, USA Today, U.S. News & World Report* and the *New York Times Book Review.* His books and tapes have received many awards including ALA Notable Book Award, Parent's Choice Gold Award, The Golden Sower Award, IRA Teacher's Choice, American Bookseller's Pick of the Lists, and the Anne Izard Storytellers Choice Award.

ALAN K. POSNER is a trial lawyer and partner at the Boston firm of Rubin and Rudman. In his practice, he faithfully attempts to follow all commandments. His previous writing credits include legal briefs to the Massachusetts Supreme Judicial Court and the First Circuit Court of Appeals.

ROSIE ROSENZWEIG is a teacher, an anthologized poet, and freelance writer whose work has appeared in *Leaving a Legacy,*

Sara's Daughters Sing, Horizons, the prayerbook *Vetaher Libanu,* and a forthcoming Rosh Chodesh anthology in press with Jason Aronson. She has just published *The Jewish Guide to Boston & New England.* She is presently writing a book about her encounters with spiritual leaders in southeast Asia.

MENORAH LAFAYETTE-LEBOVICS ROTENBERG is a psychotherapist in Teaneck, New Jersey. She holds a BHL from the Jewish Theological Seminary and an MA in Jewish History from Columbia University. In writing *midrash,* she combines her interest in psychological portraiture with her deep involvement with Judaic texts.

NANCY ELLEN ROTH, a graduate student at Baltimore Hebrew University, has been studying and *davening* for more than ten years at Fabrangen, an independent, egalitarian, participatory, *havurah* in Washington, D.C.

LUCY COHEN SCHMEIDLER worked as a computer programmer for more than thirty years before retiring to write full-time. She is the author of several poems published in *Sarah's Daughters Sing* and the first *Jewish Women's Literary Annual* as well as fantasy short stories and essays about science fiction. She lives in New York City.

HOWARD SCHWARTZ is the author of several books of fiction, including *Midrashim, Adam's Soul,* and *The Four Who Entered Paradise,* and of several books of poetry, including *Vessels, Gathering the Sparks* and *Sleepwalking Beneath the Stars.* He has also edited the anthology *Gates to the New City: A Treasury of Modern Jewish Tales,* as well as a four-volume set of Jewish folktales, which includes "Elijah's Violin," "Miriam's Tambourine," "Lilith's Cave," and "Gabriel's Palace."

BARBARA SHERROD, a writer of Regency novels, lives with her family in Fort Collins, Colorado. She and her husband are founders of Congregation Har Shalom.

MARK SOLOMON is a New York poet, teacher, and businessman. His poems are in *TriQuarterly, BOMB, Snake Nation Review, The Florida Review, The Beloit Poetry Journal,* and *Cumberland Poetry Review.* He holds an MFA in Poetry from Warren Wilson

College. His collection, *The Pleasure of a Ride,* is under considera-
tion at several publishers.

LINDA KERSH STEIGMAN, MSS, is Union of American
Hebrew Congregations Outreach Coordinator for the Pennsylvania
Council and a clinical social worker. Active in the Reform movement
since childhood, she has developed a special love for Torah study.
She would like to give special thanks to her family for increasing her
sensitivity to the voices of women and children in Torah.

SUSAN TERRIS lives in San Francisco. Her recent works in-
clude *Author! Author!* and *Nell's Quilt* (Farrar, Straus & Giroux),
Killing in the Comfort Zone (Pudding House Press), and many jour-
nal publications including *Jewish Spectator, Jewish Currents,
Midstream,* and *Tikkun.* She was a 1994 winner of the Anna Davison
Rosenberg Competition for poems on the Jewish Experience.

MARLENA THOMPSON is the Judaic Program Coordinator
at Gesher Jewish Day School in Fairfax, Virginia, where she
both writes and encourages the writing of original *midrashim.*
Thompson has also been a Hebrew language and Judaic studies
teacher for over fifteen years. She has published numerous articles on children's health, development, and education.

Index to Major Biblical Characters

ABOUT THE EDITORS

David A. Katz is currently serving as the rabbi of Temple Israel, Reform Congregation of Staten Island, New York. He received his bachelor of science and master of arts degrees in Speech/Theatre at Northwestern University. At Hebrew Union College-Jewish Institute of Religion he earned a master of arts in Hebrew Education and a master of arts in Hebrew Literature before he was ordained in New York in 1981. He is a Reform Jewish Educator (RJE), and has written in the areas of Jewish education and liturgy. He teaches theology and history at St. John's University.

Rabbi Katz lives in Staten Island with his wife and two children.

Peter Lovenheim is a writer and lawyer. His articles have appeared in *The New York Times, New York* magazine, *Moment* magazine, and the *International Jewish Monthly*. His midrash, "The Ram at Moriah," was first published in 1985 in *Genesis 2*. Mr. Lovenheim earned a bachelor of science degree in Journalism and Government, *summa cum laude*, from Boston University in 1975, and a law degree from Cornell Law School in 1978. He is author of two books on dispute resolution, *Mediate, Don't Litigate* (New York: McGraw-Hill, 1989) and *How to Mediate Your Dispute* (Berkeley: Nolo Press, 1996).

Mr. Lovenheim lives with his wife and three children in Rochester, New York.

ABOUT THE EDITORS

David A. Katz is currently serving as the rabbi of Temple Israel Reform Congregation of Staten Island, New York. He received his bachelor of science and master of arts degrees in ... at Northwestern University. After ... Gratz College, at which he ... one of Religion he earned a master of arts in Jewish education and a master of arts in History ... New York. In 1981 he ... a Reform Jewish Rabbi (JIR). and has written in the areas of Jewish Education, ... theology, and history ... Jewish University ...

Rabbi Katz lives in Staten Island with his wife and two children.

Peter Lovenheim is a writer and lawyer. His articles have appeared in The New York Times, New York magazine, Harvard magazine, and the international ... His most recent ... The Ram at Moriah ... was first published in 1995 ... He ... earned a bachelor of science degree in journalism ... also Governor's ... summa cum laude, from ... University in 1975, and a law degree from Cornell Law School in 1979. He is author of two books on dispute resolution, Mediate, Don't Litigate (McGraw Hill, 1989) and How to Manage Your Lawyer (Prometheus Press, 1996).

Mr. Lovenheim lives with his wife and three children in ... New York.